Lock Down Publications and Ca$h
Presents

I0658697

# THE MURDER QUEENS 5

## BETRAYAL IS WORSE THAN DEATH

Written By
**MICHAEL GALLON**

First Edition 2024

Printed in the United States of America

Lock Down Publications
P.O. Box 944
Stockbridge, GA 30281
www.lockdownpublications.com

Like our page on Facebook: Lock Down Publications
www.facebook.com/lockdownpublications.ldp

# Stay Connected with Us!

Text **LOCKDOWN** to 22828 to stay up-to-date with new releases, sneak peaks, contests and more…

Like our page on Facebook:
Lock Down Publications

Join Lock Down Publications/The New Era Reading Group

Visit our website:
www.lockdownpublications.com

Follow us on Instagram:
Lock Down Publications

Email Us: We want to hear from you!

# CHAPTER 1
### ACURA LEGEND!

Nicole sat behind the wheels of her brand new, cream-colored 2000 Acura Legend with the thoughts of the previous day long gone. For the very first time in her young adult life, she was on her own.

With all the money that she had accumulated during her tenure with the Florida Hot Girls, she figured that she had made enough money to purchase her a brand-new car and start her a brand-new life somewhere else for her and her precious new unborn child.

She had already marked the first thing off of her list of many things to do by purchasing her a brand-new car with her hard-earned cash. Next thing on the list was finding herself a place to stay. So, as she merged onto I-4, headed towards Daytona Beach, she began to figure out where in Daytona she would call home.

She had thought about moving to Miami, but the lifestyle down there would be too fast paced for her and her new infant on the way. And besides, she really didn't want her child growing up in such a fast-paced environment. Nor did she want to be distracted by the temptation of returning back to being a stripper. So, her choice of where to live was decided. Daytona Beach, Florida was it for her.

As she looked at facial appearance in her rearview mirror, no one could tell her that she wasn't a queen and that she couldn't be treated like one. She had even started to notice the change of her body as she sat there in the driver's seat of her automobile, weaving in and out of traffic, headed towards Daytona.

The short ride was only about forty-five minutes to an hour, so she popped opened her sunroof and let her windows down to let the wind blow through her elegant looking, Yaky, silky hair, all while thinking to herself of what the future held in store for her and her unborn child.

The only thing that mattered to her at that very moment was her getting as far away as possible from her notorious past. But there was one small problem to her doing that. And the problem was that her past wasn't going to let her get away from it.

All she needed now was a nice, quiet place to stay so that she could raise her child. She had saved up about forty thousand dollars during the time that she worked with the Hot Girls and had stolen another couple of bands from the two dead cops that she had helped dispose of. She knew that the average job wouldn't pay her the type of money that she was accustomed to making with the Florida Hot Girls, so she would definitely have to find her something that could pay her bills and keep her used to the nice lifestyle she had grown used to living.

The attitude she had now had her saying to herself, *Fuck the Florida Hot Girls and everybody associated with them!* By the time she reached Daytona, it was around three fifteen in the afternoon. She had already made a reservation at the Holiday Inn Suite Resort on the beach side, so as she pulled into the parking lot, she pulled down her Chanel shades to take in the beauty of the beach and surrounding sites. When she stepped out of her automobile, she had all eyes on her as she walked inside to check in.

The tall, lanky, young light skinned receptionist with two golds in the front of his mouth and a head full of nicely fixed dreadlocks was speechless as he watched this splendid looking young lady walk up to the front desk. Just by staring at her as she walked up to the counter had the young-aged man aroused. For a moment he fantasied. *This chick has to be a stripper, or something along that type of business.*

# CHAPTER 2

The outfit that Nicole was wearing was actually wearing her, as her body adorned a black pair of nicely fitted Apple Bottom jeans with a nice cut off Apple Bottom shirt, covering up her voluptuous breast that were mouthwatering as she stood there at the front desk of the Beach resort, smiling.

On her adorable little feet, she had on a nice pair of red Guess three-inch heels that caused her ass to sit up just right on her back as if it needed some tender loving care.

The young man couldn't keep from showing off his gold teeth as he looked at the model standing in front of him and said, "Welcome to the Holiday Inn Beach Resort. Can I help you?"

"Yes, I have a reservation here, somewhere in this big ass purse of mine," she said to the young man as she placed her shades down on the front counter of the hotel, rambling through her twelve-hundred-dollar Gucci bag.

As she frantically searched throughout her purse for her confirmation number, Daryl recited, "Okay, no need to search for your confirmation number ma'am. Give me your name so that I can look it up for you."

"Yes, it's under Ms. Nicole Vallentino." As the name rolled off of her lips, she smiled at the young man, causing him to blush as he nervously searched the computer for her name.

It also caused Nicole to stop for a minute, and relish the good times that her and I had spent together. She smiled at the thought, and then began to daydream about the times we spent together in each other's arms. It wasn't until the receptionist said. "Yes, I see where we have you booked in at one of our suites on the beach side of the hotel. Would you like the bottom floor or somewhere in between?"

Nicole snapped back to reality and replied, "Let me have the Penthouse Suite please."

"Certainly, ma'am. Do you know how long you will be staying here with us?"

"I really don't know right now. I'm moving from Orlando, so it might be a few days before I find me a nice, suitable place to reside."

"No problem, ma'am. I'll just check you in for a week and give you the winter rate so that it won't cost you as much money as the summer rate."

"Why thank you, young man," she replied as she looked at his name stitched on his white wool knitted shirt and said, "Daryl."

The young man quickly snapped his head up at Nicole and uttered, "How did you know that my name was Daryl?" She then pointed to his name on his shirt. "Oh, you saw it on my shirt. How silly of me not to realize that," Daryl muttered back to Nicole as he stood there blushing back at the young beautiful woman standing in front of him.

"Yes, young man."

"So, you staying here by yourself, ma'am?"

"Yes, I am, Daryl. Are you here by yourself?"

He was stunned by Nicole's remark and quickly caught his words. "I meant to say, do you have a boyfriend or significant other with you?"

"No, Daryl, I'm single and taking a break from men right now."

"My bad, ma'am. I must say though, you are a very beautiful woman." Daryl could sense that Nicole's heart belonged to someone else at the time and respected her wishes.

Nicole looked back at Daryl with her bright smile and sputtered, "Thank you."

"Will you be paying with cash or credit?"

"With cash, Daryl."

# CHAPTER 3

Nicole then pulled out a nice thick wad of what looked like freshly printed hundred-dollar bills. All nice and crisp as though she had printed them up that morning.

Daryl's light brown eyes enlarged at the sight of the bills inside the beautiful vixen's hand. Nicole knew that if she would have paid with her credit card, the girls or I could have traced her whereabouts which was a definite no-no due to her not wanting anyone from her past to know where she had run away to.

"How much is it, please?"

The young man was still standing there, mystified at the sight of the money, that he didn't even hear Nicole until she cleared her throat and then recited once again, this time a little louder.

"Daryl, how much is the suite?"

He quickly shook his head, causing his dreads to swing back and forth. "I'm so sorry, ma'am, your total is five hundred dollars."

Nicole then unrolled five crisp hundred dollar bills that she had withdrew from the bank before she left for Daytona.

"Thank you, ma'am. Is there anything else I can do for you today?"

"No, that will be all, young man. Once again, thank you."

"No problem, it was my pleasure," Daryl uttered as he handed her the room key and her receipt.

She received her room key and turned to walk away, leaving Daryl behind to stare at what he couldn't wait to see. Her beautiful fat round red ass, in which he could only imagine how nice it would be to have her in his bed.

While he stood there admiring Nicole walk away, he grabbed his manhood and bit down on his index finger that he had placed inside his mouth without even knowing it. "Damn, that bitch is fine as a muthafucka!" he murmured softly to himself.

Just as the pretty vixen reached the door, she turned back to Daryl and said, "How nice is the water around this time of the day?"

His eyes immediately locked on to her fat camel toe protruding through her black Apple Bottom jeans and recited, "Ahh, it's nice but how nice is that fat ass kitty cat?" he muttered under his breath.

Nicole stood there at the door smiling as she said out loud, "Excuse me, Daryl!"

"Nothing, Ms. Vallentino. I was just admiring out loud how nice you look."

"Thank you, young man. Have a nice day," she replied as she turned to walk out to her car so that she could retrieve her belongings.

Once she had everything in hand, she took the elevator up to the Penthouse Suite. The ride up to her suite took about three minutes as she reached the top of the building.

As she placed the key into the door of her suite, she couldn't wait to see what her money had paid for. The anticipation of what her room looked like kept her in suspense, as she slowly pushed the door open. When she opened the door, her anticipation had been confirmed when she walked inside the elegant looking room, which was just as big as one of the living rooms that were at the Vallentino house, where she had just left.

The spacious suite held a full kitchen, along with a nice size living room, with a dining room to go along with it.

When she opened the door of the master bedroom, she thought for a minute that she was back at the Vallentino house, but quickly got that thought out of her head when she thought about Sharon and me being together.

# CHAPTER 4
## CHILD'S LIFE!

Her bags began to weigh in her hand, so she threw her Louis Vuitton bags and Gucci purse on the bed and sat down to look out of the window of her room. While sitting there rubbing her stomach, she looked down at her belly and whispered the mere words, "Everything is going to be alright, my child, with or without your no-good father." With that said, she sat there thinking of me and wished that I could have been there with her and our unborn child.

But she knew that would never happen because I was too in love with Sharon. And if it wasn't Sharon, it was Sexy Redd, so she just sat there asking of how she could have been so careless as to give her virginity to a man who was in love with two other women. And not to mention with both being pregnant at the same time.

After wiping away a few of her salted tears, she laid back on the bed to try to get her some rest. By now the time was four fifteen in the evening. She knew that her baby was hungry, but she had no desire for food.

Her broken heart kept her from eating. All she wanted was to somehow see me or just hear my voice over the phone, as she lay there in the huge king size bed looking up into the ceiling.

While she laid there lost in space, she thought about taking a walk on the beach to help her forget about me and the past that she had just left behind. But overcome with grief and tranquility she fell comfortably into a nice deep sleep. If only she knew what was waiting for her around the corner, she might not have fallen asleep. Since she had found out about her being pregnant, she wanted nothing else to do with the Murder Queens. But little did the precious little Vixen know, it would be those same Murder Queens who she would need to save her and her unborn child's life.

# CHAPTER 5

## SAN JUAN

As the high powered, twin engine, private luxury G-4 jet plane of business tycoon Pierre Santiago flew over the Atlantic Ocean, headed towards San Juan Puerto Rico, I laid my head back, trying to sort out things in my complicated confused life, when Sexy Redd looked at me and said, "So now that we're in the air and flying under the radar, tell me what in the hell is going on, Mister!"

"Rhynyia, my darling, it's very complicated. Trust me," I replied while looking up at her standing over me with a mad ass unit covering her lovely face.

She placed her hands on those wide ass hips of hers. "Well, I'm a very complicated woman. Now tell me why in hell was half of the police force chasing you and your damn brother?"

"Damn, Rhynyia. Since you must know: First, I have no idea what they wanted; all I know right now is that someone has kidnapped Sharon and her daughter Breanna, and my unborn child." My head fell in disgust and shame.

"Who is they?"

"I don't know. When we started running I lost the call of the kidnapper and Sharon's mother."

"Well, Michael, it seems as though we have ourselves a slight problem here!" Damn, I knew that she wouldn't understand, as she looked me directly in my eyes and said, "Michael, we have to go back and rescue her!"

15

"What?" I asked with that quizzical look on my face.

"We have to go back and rescue her!" Rhynyia repeated, now looking at me as serious as a heart attack.

"You're damn right, Rhynyia!" Firstborn yelled as he jumped up out of his seat with a can of Pepsi soda in his hand.

"Wait a minute, so let me get this shit straight. So, you don't care that it's the female that's carrying my child?"

"No, silly ass man. She's carrying your child, and we definitely don't want anything to happen to her or your child."

"But what about the cops? I know that you saw them chasing us. You're not worried about your freedom?"

"Well, the way I see it is that we just have to deal with that when we get back in town."

That's when I sat down next to her and began telling her what had transpired since she had been gone. I started with how the cops were trying to extort me for some hush money, then it was some of the girls in the group who were going around killing people, calling themselves the Murder Queens. When I began telling her about the Murder Queens, she started acting funny, like there was something about those females that had her on edge. It was her body gestures that made me sense that something was very wrong.

Before I could get halfway through my story about the girls, she placed her index finger over my mouth and whispered, "Shhhhh, Michael. It's time that I tell you more about me." She sat down next to me on the leather couch.

But just as soon as she went to open her mouth, my phone began to chirp. It was a new cell company out that allowed you the ability to communicate with another by two ways, so that your call couldn't be tapped or recorded. So, it was priority for me and anyone who worked with me to have one of these phones as well. "Excuse me, Rhynyia," I said to her as I spoke into the phone. "Yeah, who is this?"

"Michael, this is Lieutenant Richards, with the Bridgeville Police department."

"Okay, and what do you guys want with my black ass?"

"We need to talk about a few things of importance."

"Okay, do I need my lawyer present with me when we meet up?" I asked as Rhynyia and Firstborn sat there with me waiting on his response.

Seconds later, he came back with, "No, this is between you and I."

"Okay, in reference to?"

"Where is my money?"

"What money?" I asked him as Firstborn placed his head in the palms of his hands.

"The money that you owed to my two homicide detectives that you had murdered! I hope you just don't think that it was those two fools who needed their palms greased."

Now I was really puzzled. "So, what are you trying to say, detective?"

"I really don't won't to talk over the phone. Why don't you just turn that nice jet plane around so that we can work something out. Hell, I don't need you in jail. I need you out so that you can keep paying me."

"Fuck!" I shouted.

"So, Mister Michael Vallentino, are we going to meet so that we can make this all disappear?"

"I'll meet with you once I return to Orlando in a week."

Rhynyia slowly reached out for my hand so that she could comfort me through the conversation.

"Okay. Michael, you might want to make that sooner than later, because I wouldn't want anything to happen to your beautiful Ms. Sharon Conoly!"

As he uttered Sharon's name, chills ran through my body, as I stood to my feet. "What? How in the hell do you know about her being kidnapped?"

"Damn, son. Who in the hell do you think has her!"

# CHAPTER 6

## RHYNYIA TOO!

I stood there with a dismal, dismayed look upon my face, staring at Firstborn, then at Sexy Redd. I then held the phone to my mouth and said, "So, it was you who kidnapped her?"

"I have to have something to bargain with, young man, don't you think?"

"So, you were the officer that tried to prevent my brother and I from getting on the plane?"

"Yes. Now enough with the questions. Turn the damn plane around and wait for me to call you again with instructions on where and when to bring me my damn money! If not, the bitch is dead!"

Right after he had uttered those words through my phone, Rhynyia was up and yelling to Miguel, the pilot. "Miguel, turn the plane around immediately! We're going back to Orlando!"

"What about your father, Princess?" Maria shouted as she jumped up from her seat.

"I will call him and explain later. Right now my sisters and I have something of importance to take care of!"

I was still standing there with my phone in my hand asking myself, *Her sisters? I never knew about her having any damn sisters back in Orlando!* It was then that my conscience looked at me from across the seats of the plane and said, *I told your black ass that she was quick on her feet! Didn't I?*

"What does she mean, her sisters?"

He then smiled back at me with that devilish grin that he always held on his face. He paused for a minute or two and then he took out a cigar from his left suit pocket and slowly placed it inside his mouth. He then held his head down as he flipped open a gold lighter and lit the cigar. As he brought his head back up numbly, he said, "She's talking about her sisters in crime."

"What sisters in crime, dammit?" I cried.

"The Murder Queens! Smart ass!"

I fell down in the seat and uttered, "Damn!"

Meanwhile, Rhynyia had been in the cock pit, checking with Miguel about when we would arrive back in Orlando.

When she returned, I looked her directly in her eyes and said, "Rhynyia, is there something that you want to tell me now?"

She looked at me with her cute brown eyes and said, "No, but I do have something to show you," as she sat down beside me once again. She pulled her Helen Saint Claire skirt to the side, revealing a small portion of her very pleasing looking shaved vagina, that her thong could barely keep hidden away from my staring eyes.

As I leaned in and looked a little closer on her inner thigh, there it was. That same tattoo that the four other girls in my group had in the same damn place. It simply read what I already had known but tried to convince myself that it wasn't true. "Damn, Rhynyia to was a part of the group of females that the world had grown to know only as the infamous Murder Queens.

# CHAPTER 7
## FROM NICOLE!

Mignon woke up around eight thirty that Monday morning. She couldn't believe how peaceful she had slept throughout the night without any difficulties or bad dreams. As she sat up in her nice king-size bed, the first thing that popped in her head was what time would Firstborn and I be leaving for the airport. With that lingering over her head, she searched her bedroom floor for her slippers so she could search the house for answers.

After throwing on something nice to wear downstairs, she walked through the hallway searching for who else might be in the massive structure. First, she went by Strawberry's room and found her lying there sleeping with saliva oozing from her open mouth.

"Ew, Strawberry, close your mouth, girl!" she said as she closed the door back.

Next, she walked up on Entyce's room where she found Reese and Entyce fast asleep hugging on one another while they dreamed of having their own place one day. Then it was off to see what her best friend Nicole was up to. But as she got to Nicoles door, she was surprised to find the door slightly ajar. "Nicole, are you awake?" She slowly pushed open Nicole's bedroom door. When she finally found herself standing inside Nicole's room, she was stunned. No she was baffled. "Oh my God, the crazy ass bitch is gone!" Mignon turned and quickly ran downstairs to see if maybe Nicole was just somewhere else inside the house. But after frantically searching throughout the house, to no avail, her dear friend Nicole was nowhere to be found.

*Damn, I sure hope to God that this crazy ass bitch hasn't went and done something stupid or deadly,* Mignon recited to herself as she walked into the kitchen to find her something to drink.

While pouring her a tall cold glass of orange juice, she started playing back the events and words Nicole had said over the last few days about getting rid of Sharon. As she stood there pondering over those awful words through her head, she spotted a note sitting on the counter addressed to me, from Nicole.

# CHAPTER 8
## CHANNEL ELEVEN!

*To: My Dearest Michael,*

*I hope that this letter finds you in sound health, body and mind. I, on the other hand, has lived to have had better days. Let me cut straight to the chase, Michael. I've tried to deal with the painful stress of loving you, but you haven't done the same for me. So, with that said, I've decided that a different environment would be more suitable for my child and I. Please don't try to find me, I'm moving on from you and this group, along with the previous lifestyle that I have grown accustomed to living. Once I have our child, my lawyers and I will get in touch with you. Then and only then will I get in touch with you! There was no way that I was going to sit around and watch you sleep around with whomever it was you decided on sleeping with. Nor was I sticking around for you to one day choose someone else other than me as your wife. I've learned so much by being around you and the others. Let them know that I will always think of them, as I know that they will always think of me. Michael, please remember what I told you about you being the first and only man that I have ever slept with. That meant a lot to me. I always thought that the man who I allowed to have my virginity would eventually be the man I married. Not only is that not possible now, but you have showed me that all I ever was to you was a nice piece of ass. Goodbye, Michael, and always be safe. I never imagined that I would fall in love with*

*you, but I did. Now I have to live the rest of my life trying to*
*get over you.*
  *With All of My Love,*
  *Nicole Diameshia Jackson*
  *P. S. Let Mignon and the rest of the Murder Queens know*
*that we will always remain Sisters 4 Life! I cannot control*
*my tears from rolling down my face.*

With tears streaming down the face of Mignon, all she could do was imagine the pain that Nicole was going through all by herself. She stood silent for a moment and asked herself, with all the hurt Nicole was going through, would she actually bring any harm to Sharon? She was still standing there dormant, while speculating that thought over and over in her head, when she was suddenly startled by Strawberry.

"Hey, you. You're up early aren't you?" Strawberry asked Mignon as she pulled at the door of the refrigerator.

Mignon quickly wiped her face before Strawberry noticed her crying and realizing that she had a soft side to her after all. "Oh, hey girl, what are you doing up so early?" She wiped the last dried tear off of her red cheek.

"Girl, please, it's already ten fifteen. What's up?"

"Look!"

"What's this?" Strawberry asked Mignon as she reached out for the letter.

"A letter from Nicole. Here. Read it."

Strawberry took the letter and began reading it. Within minutes she too had tears well up in the bottom of her eyes. While holding back the onslaught of her emotions, she gently placed the letter back on the countertop, and then looked in the face of Mignon. "Hey, you don't think that she did anything crazy with Sharon, do you?"

"Only time will tell. Right now we have to get in touch with Mike and let him know that she has left the group."

Two minutes later, Entyce was running down the stairs screaming. "Hey, guys! Turn on the news! Channel eleven!"

# CHAPTER 9
## POLICE AT THE DOOR!

All three of the lovely ladies ran into the living room area, trying to see what all the commotion was about. "Move, Strawberry!" Mignon shouted as she reached for the remote.

"Damn, Mignon, my bad!" Strawberry replied as she squatted down in front of the television screen.

The screen then brightly emerged with the face of the elegant looking Camelia Fields, news anchor for Channel Eleven News. "Good morning. This is Camelia Fields with breaking news from Channel Eleven! We are going live to Tasha Willis with this breaking news report."

"Thank you, Camelia. This is Tasha Willis reporting for Channel Eleven News. We're here with the family of Sharon Conoly, who along with her three-year-old daughter, have been missing since late Saturday evening. This is a photo of what the two looked like. The police and surrounding neighbors have been frantically searching the area for her and her daughter since Saturday. They had just finished up with the funeral of her late cousin, who was shot and killed about three weeks ago, when they were reported missing the next day. Her car and personnel items were found along Highway Fifty, with the car door left open and keys still inside the car ignition. Her mother was called by the local police, who at that time had put out a missing person's report as to the whereabouts of these two individuals. If anyone has any information as to where they might be, please contact your local Crime Stoppers with the information. I'm Tasha Willis reporting for Channel Eleven News. Back to you Camelia."

After the girls saw the news broadcast, they immediately pondered the thought of Nicole having something to do with the disappearance of Sharon and her young daughter, when they heard a loud knock at the front door.

"Now who in the hell could this be, knocking all hard like they're the damn police or something!" Strawberry uttered as she strutted to the front door to open it. Just as she reached the front door, she happened to take a quick peak out of the window. After witnessing who it was, she quickly turned around to say, "Hey, it is the damn police at the door!" she sputtered with her mouth all twisted up.

"Well open the damn door before they knock it off of the hinges!" Mignon yelled back.

The door slowly crept open with Strawberry saying, "Yes, can I help you?"

"Good morning, ma'am. Is Michael Vallentino here?" the tall white officer who stood around six foot six with dark black hair and a very deep black beard said to Strawberry.

Strawberry then turned to Mignon who had stepped up behind her and said, "Hey, is Mike here?"

Mignon quickly stepped in front of Strawberry and said, "No, sir, he left for the airport a few hours ago."

"Do you know where he's flying to?" the one officer asked as both side-stepped Mignon and walked inside the house.

"No, sir. Wherever they're going, it had to do with business."

"You said they. Who else would be traveling with Mr. Vallentino?" the officer asked Mignon, who already had given up too much information.

"Him and his brother, sir!" Entyce replied as she stepped forward wearing some shorts with no panties on. Her round, plump ass hung out of her tight ass shorts, along with her titties protruding through her cut-off Florida Hot Girl t-shirt.

# CHAPTER 10
## CUBAN SANDWICH!

As the two officers stood there gazing at how gorgeous all three women looked, they didn't know what to do— either search the house or violate the women standing before them.

*Damn, this nigga must be the black Hugh Heffner with all of this fine ass pussy running around this big ass house!* the other officer said to himself.

The officer stood a mere six foot four and weighed around two hundred and twenty pounds, sporting a black suit that looked like he had purchased it from Walmart's clearance rack. He had dark brown, shifty eyes and sandy blonde hair, along with a slight scar along the right side of his face. He had never thought about having sex with a black girl, but as fine as those young ladies were looking, it started to cross his mind.

He had a very deep, raspy voice that stopped the ladies dead in their tracks when he asked them, "Listen, ladies, my partner and I don't want to waste any of your time, but do anyone of you nice looking ladies know where Mr. Vallentino and his brother might be traveling to?"

Strawberry cleared her throat. "Like my sister just told you two white police officers, they are at the airport. That's all we know."

"Okay, ladies. Thank you very much for your help. Is there a number where we might be able to reach him?"

"He just changed phone providers to this new phone company by the name of Nextel. His number is 407-321-5242. And his chirp number is 107-6543-2121," Mignon replied.

"Thank you ladies for your time and help. If he calls you all before we get in touch with him, please give him my number." The lead officer then handed the card to the ladies as him and his partner walked out to their black Chevy Impala, headed for the airport.

"Damn, you bitches sure as shell gave them two ugly ass cops a lot of fucking information!" Strawberry said to Entyce and Mignon, who were standing there looking lost and out of place.

"Listen, it was just his phone number. Hell what has he did that they are gonna arrest him for anyway?" Entyce screamed at Strawberry, while following her into the kitchen.

"It's not that, Entyce. It's just the point that you and Mignon gave out too much critical information. What if Mike didn't want them crackers to know anything? Hell, all we know is that he just went to Puerto Rico to get away from all of the noise going on around here!"

"Better yet, what if all this was planned ahead by Mike and Sexy Redd?" Mignon replied, while looking like she had unearthed a great mystery.

"What are you talking about now, Mignon?" Strawberry asked while pulling out some items from the fridge, so that she could make her one of her special homemade deluxe Cuban sandwiches.

"Remember that day at the Olive Garden, when Sexy Redd said that her and Michael were going on vacation?"

"Yeah, so what?" Entyce asked, while observing Strawberry prepare her sandwich.

"That's it. Mike knew that he would be leaving and Rhynyia was coming back to get him," Mignon said as she watched Strawberry stuff her sandwich into her mouth.

"So, bitch, you're not going to fix our hungry ass one of those big ass deluxe sandwiches that you just sat your apple-headed ass down and made for yourself?"

"Nah. If y'all hungry ass hoes were hungry, you should have fixed yourselves one instead of running your mouths to those damn cops!" Strawberry replied, as she took her third bite out of her sandwich.

# CHAPTER 11
## CRANIUM!

Mignon and Entyce had their eyes glued on the sandwich that was coming out of Strawberry's mouth, when Entyce looked back over at Mignon and said, "So, Mignon, you actually think that Mike and Rhynyia were planning this shit, all along?"

"Man, y'all hoes tripping. How in the hell did he have this planned? He wasn't aware of Rhynyia's brother getting killed," Strawberry replied.

"Man, forget all of that. All we know is that Nicole's ass is gone and the fucking police are looking for Mike. Not to mention, Sharon and her precious lil' girl are missing!" Mignon said while placing some lettuce and mustard on her sandwich that she had tried to duplicate from watching Strawberry.

Inside Lieutenant Richards' black Chevy Impala, he had just placed a call to one of his officers. "This is Lieutenant Richards. I need Chris, Kyle and Roman to meet me over at Orlando International Airport, immediately. I think that our dear friend Michael Vallentino is trying to leave the country with our money. I have too much invested in this lil' scheme to see it all go down the drain because we let ourselves get outsmarted by some wannabe pimp."

"I agree. I need that money for the new house I'm having built off of John Young Parkway," an officer said on the other line.

"Once we get our money, we're going to have to kill his precious lil' bitch so that we can cover our trail," Lieutenant Richards said back into the phone as he was weaving in and out of traffic with his siren on.

As he hung up the phone, his partner who was agitatedly sitting across from him looked over in his direction. "So, what's the plan once we get to the airport?"

"To be honest with you, I want to go back to that house and have my way with Mignon!" Lieutenant Richards replied while grabbing his crotch, causing a wicked smile to emerge across his face.

"I was thinking the same thing, but I want me a nice bowl of some Strawberries, if you get my drift," his partner replied, while showing off his few gold teeth. "Have you ever been with a black chick before?" his partner asked, while he sat there still daydreaming about being with Strawberry.

"Nah, I've had a couple of my friends back at the Academy tell me that's it mind-blowing to have sex with a sister, though."

"Well, I've had the pleasure of being with a few of them fine ass sisters, and let me tell you, when they fuck you, they really fuck you. It can become very addictive if you're not careful," his partner said while Lieutenant Richards merged onto the expressway, trying to get to the airport before the plane took off. "So how was it?" Lieutenant Richards asked his partner.

Officer John Hatfield responded, "If I tell you how it was, I would have to kill you after I told you."

John replied while laughing at his remark. "Well, I guess I'll find out after I fuck his pretty lil' model-looking bitch Sharon. Then take her out back and shoot the pretty lil' black bitch in the back of her cranium. The way whomever it was killed those two dumb ass cops that I had working for me!"

# CHAPTER 12
## UNEXPECTED QUEST!

Nicole woke up around six that evening, craving something to feed her and her unborn child. She hadn't eaten since earlier that day and knew that it would only be a matter of time before she really felt the hunger pains from inside the digestive system of her frail stomach. First, she thought of having some room service bring her up something to eat until she looked outside of her penthouse suite and saw how beautiful it was becoming, with the sun setting far off in the distance. So, she decided to venture outside to find something while enjoying the beautiful ocean side view at the same time. As she looked at the attire that adorned her splendid-looking body, she decided to change into something more suitable for her stroll down the boardwalk. When she left the Vallentino house earlier that day, she only took enough clothes to get her by for a couple of days. So, before she checked into the hotel, she stopped by the mall on International Drive and picked up a few more outfits.

After looking over her new attire, she picked out a pair of Dior jeans and a nice shirt to go along with the ensemble. To keep her warm, she threw on a nice black Baby Phat hoodie. She walked over to her mirror and uttered to herself, "Okay, that's my girl. Now, only if Michael could see me now. Oh well. One man's loss is another man's treasure." She then grabbed some money from her Gucci purse and headed for the door.

Just as she was closing her door, she heard her room phone ring but thought nothing of it. She just let it continue to ring. When she reached the elevators, she pushed the button and waited for the door to open. As soon as the elevator door opened and she stepped on, the elevator door next to the one she got on, opened up with an unexpected guest stepping off on her floor.

Stepping off onto the ground floor, she headed towards her new automobile thinking that she was going to drive to a nearby restaurant. She stood at her car door, hesitating for a brief moment as she thought, *Since it's such a nice evening, I might as well walk to help ease my mind.* She then pulled the hoodie over her nice hairdo and started strolling towards the Red Lobster, while the unexpected guest pulled out a hotel key and entered her room with his weapon drawn.

# CHAPTER 13
## DEATH CERTIFICATE!

The elegantly styled penthouse suite was quiet, just the way the assailant wanted it to be, so that he could catch his subject alone and alarmed to see him. First, he went inside the master bedroom. When he didn't see her there, he gently walked into the bathroom, thinking that she might be in there soaking in the bath tub. He instantaneously pushed the door of the bathroom back, gun drawn, ready to strike at the first sight of her. But to his surprise, she wasn't there. He then went through her Gucci purse, looking for any clues that might help lead to where she might have gone. He found nothing as he angrily threw her purse back down on the king-sized bed. Seconds later, he journeyed back through the living room, still probing for clues. He was determined to find anything that could help lead him to find her.

After about twenty minutes of turning her suite upside down, he decided to go back downstairs and see if she was in the hotel lobby or gift shop, purchasing something nice for herself. Time was of the essence and he knew that as soon as he got rid of her, he would have to get rid of the three remaining Murder Queens as well, in order for him to receive his money for killing the women responsible for taking out his homies, brother and nephew back in Jacksonville. Somehow their secret had been revealed to the older brother of the guy who had been brutally murdered over the weekend. That's when Marquise had hired the assailant known as Death Certificate to handle his dirty work.

Death Certificate had the look of a New York model, but the heart of a cold-blooded killer for hire. He stood six foot five weighing around two hundred and forty-five pounds, with long dreadlocks that he always kept tied up on his head, resembling the rapper *Gunplay*. He also adorned a full beard to hide the scars on the side of his face that he obtained while being deployed in Operation Desert Storm. He was a highly skilled, trained killer that the Military let slip out of their hands.

As Death Certificate stepped off the elevator onto the ground floor, no one could tell that he was a hired killer by the way he was dressed. He was decked out in a dark brown pair of Karl Kani jeans, with a pair of dark brown Timberland Boots with a light brown Karl Kani sweater to set off his outfit.

As he walked throughout the hotel lobby, headed for the door, he lightly bumped into a beautiful young female coming through the door.

"Oh, excuse me, sir, I'm so clumsy," the young woman said to him as she bent over to pick up her purse that he had knocked out of her hand.

"No problem, ma'am. It was my fault. I wasn't paying any attention to where I was going," Death Certificate uttered back to the young lady as she stood there smiling at him in amazement as to how handsome he looked to her.

He gave the splendid-looking woman a quick smile and continued walking away, looking for his pregnant victim. But little did Death Certificate know that the woman he had just bumped into was also there to kill someone, too. And that someone was none other than Death Certificate himself.

# CHAPTER 1
## RED LOBSTER!

The bright skinned young lady quickly spotted Daryl from the corner of her eye staring at her. She vaguely walked up to the front counter with her gorgeous smile beaming about her face and said, "Excuse me young man. Have you seen this female?"

Daryl took the photo out of her hand, smiling as he looked over the photo of Nicole and some girls standing in what looked like bathing suits inside someone's house. "Ah, yes, she checked in here earlier today. I knew she had to be a stripper, or something along that line of work!" Daryl said as he looked back into the face of the young lady who had handed it to him.

"Okay, is she still here?"

"I think that I saw her leave about forty minutes ago, dressed in some nice fitting ass jeans with a black hoodie covering her head."

"Thank you, young man."

"Do you need a room as well, ma'am?" Daryl asked the young lady as she turned to walk away.

"No, I'm good. I'm just trying to find my sister before it's too late," the young lady uttered as she hastily walked out of the door, headed to the automobile outside waiting for her return.

"Damn, she was just as fine as Ms. Vallentino was. And that was her sister? Wow. I just wish I could have one of them for myself," Daryl mumbled to himself.

Once outside, the young woman stepped back inside her vehicle and said, "It's a damn shame that we have to kill such a nice-looking young man before he kills us!"

"I hear you, girl. It seems as though we got here just in the nick of time before he took out our precious lil' sister, Nicole," Strawberry voiced as she went to start the vehicle in which they were seated in.

"Nicole has to be walking somewhere down that way, because there is more to Daytona in that direction," Entyce recited as she pulled down her Gucci shades to get a good look at what was up ahead.

"Do any of you know what Nicole even has on so that we could spot her?" Strawberry asked as she made a right onto Highway A-1-A.

"The front desk clerk said that she had on a nice pair of black jeans and a black hoodie over her head."

"Damn, he was jocking our girl mighty hard if he noticed her like that," Strawberry replied while driving down the highway.

While Mignon and Strawberry went back in forth, Entyce sat in the backseat of the car looking over their arsenal of weapons to choose from when she came across a smooth looking Colt 45 automatic. "Damn, when did we get this nice ass Colt 45 automatic?" Entyce asked the ladies as she marveled at the weapon.

"Girl, we picked that up two weeks ago. I thought you knew," Strawberry replied while turning back around to keep her eye on the steady traffic in front of her.

"I must have not been paying any attention when you guys bought this one," Entyce uttered as she pulled out the clip of the weapon.

As Strawberry continued driving slowly down Highway A-1-A, Mignon spotted Nicole walking into Red Lobster, minutes later, all by herself. "Hey, there she is right there!"

"Where?" Strawberry yelled, sounding all excited.

"She's right there, walking into Red Lobster." Mignon then pointed over to Nicole as she darted inside Red Lobster, not realizing that she was being followed by two groups of people.

# CHAPTER 15
## DAYTONA!

Entyce sat up straight in the backseat of the vehicle and shouted, "I see her! Damn my girl looks nice as hell in those Djor jeans." A single tear began to snake down her right cheek as Entyce sat there overcome with joy to see her closest friend in the group safe and sound.

"Strawberry, whip this muthafucker around to the back. Entyce, you go inside and sit down with her while I try to distract the fine ass nigga who wants to kill all of us!"

Entyce then jumped out of the vehicle and fleetly went inside Red Lobster looking for Nicole. "Okay, now where did she go?" Entyce mumbled to herself. "There she is!" Entyce uttered as she spotted Nicole sitting near the rear of the nice establishment, by herself.

"Excuse me, ma'am. Do you need a seat?" the hostess asked Entyce, who was caught by surprise.

"Ah, yeah, can you sit me over there behind the young lady in the back, sitting by herself?"

"Yes, ma'am, follow me please."

"Hey, hold up chick. I tell you what. I'll sit myself. I want to surprise my girl." Entyce uttered.

"Why of course, ma'am. Do you need a menu?"

"Yes, thank you." Entyce quickly grabbed the menu and opened it up, walking in the direction of Nicole, concealing her face so that Nicole didn't see her.

As Nicole sat there at her table looking over the menu, she already knew what she wanted to eat before she even sat down. So, to kill time waiting on her waitress, she pulled out her cellphone and dialed the number to her mother.

The phone rang three times before her mother answered. "Hello."

"Hey, ma," Nicole said to her mother as she sat there twirling her index finger through her hair.

"Is this you, Nicole?" her mother asked as her voice cracked with excitement, since it had been a while since she had heard Nicole's voice.

"Yes, ma' am. Who else would it be?" Nicole replied while trying to hold back her emotions since she was hearing her mother's voice for the very first time in months.

"Nicole, where are you and how are you doing?"

"I'm fine, mother. I'm in Daytona looking for a nice place to live. Have you been getting the money I've been sending you?"

"Daytona, and you were the one who has been sending me all of that money?"

"Yes, ma'am, Daytona. And I just figured since I had a job that I would help you with your bills."

"Nicole, with all of that money you've been sending me I have had way too much to pay these lil' small bills I have. And where in the world have you been getting that much money from?"

Before Nicole could answer her mother, the waitress came over to her table and asked her, "Are you ready to order, ma'am?"

"Hold on, ma. Yes, let me have the Ultimate Feast, please."

"And what would you like to drink, ma'am?"

"I'll have the Raspberry Lemonade."

"Would you like the soup or salad, ma'am?"

"Let me have the salad, along with those cheese biscuits."

"Okay, ma'am, I'll be right back with your order."

"Thank you, ma'am. Ma," Nicole uttered, as she placed the phone back to her ear.

"Yes, Nicole, I see that you must be doing very well for yourself."

"I'm doing okay, mother."

"So, why haven't you been by here to see me?"

"I've been real busy these last few months, ma. I just bought me a car, and now I'm here in Daytona, trying to find a place to stay."

"Why Daytona? Why couldn't you have moved closer to me?"

"Your absolutely right, ma, but I think a different environment would be better for me and my baby."

# CHAPTER 16
## CHIRP NUMBER!

Nicole's mother was startled when she heard her young virgin daughter utter the word *baby*. "Baby? Oh my God, don't tell me that you're pregnant."

"Yes, ma'am," Nicole replied with a slight bit of hesitation in her light voice.

"Are you and the baby's father together? Because I would hate to see another black child brought into the world without a mother and father to raise the child."

Nicole hesitated once again for a brief moment, then she replied with a little white lie. "Yes, ma'am, we're together."

"Well, let me speak to the young man, since you all are together," Nicole's mother asked her, while she sat there caught off guard by her question.

"He went to the restroom, ma."

"Well, why didn't I hear you place an order for him?"

"He ordered before he went to the restroom."

"Whatever, Nicole. You always were a good ass liar, just like your father. The man could tell a lie before his mouth opened."

"See, ma, there you go again, and you wonder why I never call or come home. It's because you always say that I remind you of my father. It's not my fault that he wasn't an honest man and cheated on you!"

All the while Nicole sat there on the phone with her mother, discussing their torrid past, she didn't see the nice looking man standing there watching her every move. Neither did she see Entyce sitting behind her, watching the man watching her. By now Strawberry and Mignon were out back waiting to hear from Entyce, who was on the inside waiting before she made her move to rescue Nicole.

Three hours earlier, Lieutenant Richards stood next to his partner, watching the private G-4 jet ascend into the blue skies of the clouds that were starting to darken. He turned slightly to his partner, hesitating for a moment and then said, "Damn, there goes my damn money." He then blew out billows of smoke into the air from his Marlboro cancer stick.

"So, how much money do you think is left of what was taken?"

"Not enough for my kid's graduation or my goddamn mortgage!" Lieutenant Richards was so heated that saliva sprayed from his mouth like a water hose, splashing his partner's reddish beat face while expressing his anger about his share of the money.

His partner, John Hatfield, understood his anger because he was feeling the same way. He wiped his face with the sleeve of his shirt as they walked to the cruiser, and then said to his partner, "So, you're just going to spit in my damn face and not even apologize?"

Lieutenant Richards swatted his young partner on his back. "Please, excuse me. I didn't mean any harm. It's just a lot to take in when you have a quarter of a million dollars fly away, right in your face, and there's not a damn thing you can do about it. Look. Look at our damn money!" Lieutenant Richards shouted while pointing at the G-4 flying away.

They then turned around and chuckled about what had just happened as Lieutenant Richards took out his Nextel phone and abruptly punched in the chirp number of none other than—

# CHAPTER 17
## ASPARAGUS!

As Sharon rolled over on the small, piss-stained, twin sized bed she laid on, she looked over at her daughter Breanna, who was still fast asleep. She sat hopelessly, wondering what the fate of her and her small daughter would be, along with her unborn child. Would Michael come to rescue them in time, or would he be too late? She reflected on what caused her and her daughter to be kidnapped by whomever it was and why. Her worst fear was the dreaded thought of her kidnappers doing to her what had happened to her cousin Do-Dirty and her uncle, the Notorious Bernard Fats Walker. She didn't know how long they had been in the small cubical of a room, all she knew was that they were being held against their will. Her and her daughter were tired, hungry and scared of what her captors had in store for her and her unborn son.

As she began to search throughout the small stale-smelling room for clues to where they were, she noticed that the windows in the room where all blackened out so that she wasn't able to see out of them. She noticed the one door that led into the room, so she knew that her only way out was through that door, in which she viciously began pounding on.

The door felt like steel as she cried out loud. "Damn, this is some real fucked up ass shit!" She then continued beating on the door until she couldn't bear the pain. She fell to the hard cement floor with tears flowing down her once beautiful face, which was now stricken with stress and depression of not knowing her small family's fate. As she crawled up in a ball like position on the cold, cement floor, she screamed out loud, hoping that she would be rescued before it was too late.

Minutes later, she heard keys fumbling in the door. She immediately stood to her feet to see who or what would emerge from beyond the steel door.

Once the door dully slid open, a slim shadow of a woman appeared in all black, carrying a nice tray of what smelt like food. "Here is something to eat and stop banging on the damn door. No one is going to hear you out here in these woods anyway!" the woman said as she slid over the tray of food to her.

"Who are you, and why are you holding us against our will?" Sharon shouted back at the woman as the woman was trying to close the door behind her.

The woman rashly turned back towards Sharon and said, "It doesn't matter who I am. What matters the most is that your boyfriend gets here with what he owes us before it's too late for you and your precious little girl," the woman uttered to Sharon as she slammed the steel door.

"Fuck. What does Michael have us involved in?" Sharon yelled as she slammed her injured hand down onto the bed, causing Breanna to wake up out of her deep sleep.

She then went to the small wooden table where the tray with the food had been placed. Upon opening it, she was somewhat surprised to find several pieces of fried chicken, mashed potatoes and gravy, with some nice long pieces of asparagus to go along with the meal.

As she slowly inspected the food before eating it, she lethargically picked up a stem of the asparagus and said to herself, "What in the hell is this shit? Black people don't eat no damn asparagus. These have to be some snob-nose fucking crackers who have us locked up down here in this make-shift basement."

# CHAPTER 18
### WHO'S YANI?

By now, Sharon was starving and she knew that she had to eat something. Not just for her but for the sake of her unborn child. She silently prayed over the full course meal, and then numbly nibbled on a piece of chicken.

As she took a few bites of the food, Breanna slid over to the side of her.

She let the small piece of chicken fall to the plate as she grabbed her daughter and pulled her small body in towards her, and then squeezed her tightly, not wanting to let go. She then placed her lips up against her young daughter's ear and whispered, "Don't worry, baby. Michael will be here soon to take us back home."

"Mommy, I'm hungry and it's cold in here." Breanna mumbled.

"I know, baby. Here, eat a piece of this chicken." Sharon then placed a part of the blanket from the bed around Breanna as they sat there and ate the food that was prepared for them.

On the plane, I was still getting over the fact that Rhynyia wanted to go back and rescue Sharon, but what bothered me the most was finding out that she was a part of the Murder Queens. "Okay, if we're going to do this I have to make a quick phone call," I uttered to Rhynyia as she was sitting next to me in deep thought about what she was going to tell her father about her delay back home. I stood up and dialed the 305 number and waited for her to answer.

She must have seen that it was me calling and answered on the very first ring. "Hello, Michael."

"Hello to you also my good friend. How in the hell are you?"

"I'm fine, my bruda. Couldn't be better," she replied in her cute native tongue.

"Listen, something of importance has come up, and we're going to need your expertise to help us skin a cat."

"Me good with dat, bruda."

"Cool, go ahead and pack a few things for a few days. We're about an hour away from Miami. We'll pick you up from the airport. Hold on one minute while I find out what hanger to have you meet us at. Rhynyia, is there a hanger we can have Yani to meet us at?"

"Yani? Who's Yani?"

"The chick I'm on the phone with. I'll explain that later; now is there a hanger?"

"Yes, my father has a private hanger at Miami International. Tell her to be at hanger sixteen."

"Okay, Yani, meet us at hanger sixteen. See you in about an hour."

"Peace, bruda, and remember, no worries," Yani uttered as she disconnected our phone call.

Just as soon as I hung up, Rhynyia looked deep into my eyes while staring me down. "So, who is Yani, Michael?"

"She's an old friend with some very nice skills when it comes to making someone disappear," I answered, cutting her a wicked grin.

"Whatever, Michael. I don't know why you had to call her. Hell, I'm back now, and I'm all you are gonna need to get the job done." She she stood up to retrieve a bag from the overhead compartment.

It was plain to see how nice her ass was shaped through here Helen Saint Claire skirt. Firstborn looked over at me and said, "Damn, boy, you have all the luck with the ladies. She's so damn fine that I would lick the crack of her ass right about now." He was licking his lips and rubbing his hands together.

Rhynyia sat back down with a black carrying case engraved with her name on it.

I was just about to check Firstborn's ass when she popped open the bag and pulled out a brand spanking new chrome plated four nickel. She looked up at me smiling and uttered, "I never leave home without my baby."

I took a good look at her new toy and then got back to Firstborn for his nasty ass comment.

# CHAPTER 19

## LIKE SHARON!

It took me a few seconds to think of what I wanted to say to my brother for making that remark about Rhynyia. But after a minute or two I realized that he was only saying what ever came to his thick ass head. "Yo, could you please be a little bit respectful when it comes to my lady!"

He just sat there with a silly ass smirk on his face. It wasn't until Rhynyia cut in. "Now don't you get your brother started, Firstborn. You and every other man on the planet knows that all of this belongs to Michael Vallentino."

"I know, Redd. I was just messing with his lil' young, jealous ass. You know, trying to see what his reaction was going to be." Now, don't get me wrong, my brother was smooth and all, but not smooth enough when it came to acquiring nice, beautiful women.

Many people would always say that he was so smooth that he could talk a cat down from off of a fish truck, but when it came to talking to the women, he just couldn't articulate his words in the right sentence. Me, on the other hand, I could talk the panties right off of a woman without even thinking about it.

"So, Rhynyia, what did you decide to tell your father as to why we had to return back to Orlando?"

"One thing about my father, Michael, is that whatever it is that I have to tell him, he will agree to it. Why, because I'm his first child, which means I hold the key to his heart.

Second thing is that I'm grown and I make my own decisions on what I do with my life."

My brother looked over at me with his mouth turned up. "Well, I guess she told you."

"Whatever."

"Firstborn, don't be so hard on Michael. He still has a lot to learn when it comes to me," Rhynyia replied, laughing.

Maria walked back from the cock pit area. "Princess, we shall be landing in about thirty minutes."

"Thank you, Maria. We will only be here long enough for Yani to get on board. As soon as she's on board, have Miguel get us back in the air, headed to Orlando as soon as possible."

"Yes, Princess. I shall inform him right now." Maria smiled and darted back to the cock pit area.

"Michael, excuse me while I go call my father to let him know that we will be delayed for a few days or so." She stood up and walked away as my rock headed ass brother continued watching her ass sway from one to the next.

"Damn, baby brother, I didn't know that she was that damn fine!"

"Thanks, Firstborn," I replied as I stared out of the window, thinking of Sharon and Breanna, not to mention my unborn son that she was caring.

"For real, son, what are you going to do?"

"About what?" I said as I laid my chin into my hand.

He turned sideways in the plane. "Mike, you have her and Sharon, and I know that you haven't forgot about that one lil' crazy ass girl Nicole."

As soon as the thought of all of the women put together, my mind went a drift on what I was going to do about those three beautiful women. I hadn't spoken to Nicole since Thursday or Friday. Once she saw me with Mo Money over the weekend, her whole demeanor changed towards me, and come to think about it, Nicole barely spoke to me at all.

"Hey, let me ask you something before it slips my mind?"

"What is it now, Firstborn?" I said as I turned my head and looked at him with a do not disturb sign expression on my face.

"I might not be the sharpest nail in the toolbox, but doesn't Rhynyia look a bit much like your girl Sharon?"

# CHAPTER 20
### PRINCESS RHYNYIA!

I took a long look back at my brother before uttering, "Yeah, they do, sometimes. But there's no way they can be related."

"Damn being related. They look like they can actually be sisters."

"Damn, Firstborn. Related means being sisters or even cousins."

"Nigga, I know what related means. What? You think I'm retarded or something?" he angrily replied.

"Naw, my bad. Just forget about it." I then stared back out of the window, placing my head in the palm of my hand and began to try and sort things through my mind.

It then dawned on me that Nicole hadn't even called me. I hoped that she was okay and could only imagine how she would feel once she saw Sexy Redd back at the house so soon.

Moments later, the private luxury G-4 jet plane was about to land at Miami International airport. I had to make sure that I had the right people behind me to take down a group of corrupt cops. I knew by asking Yani for her help, I was about to put together a team of elite individuals who didn't fear death at all. These individuals would look death directly in the face and say, "Not to day death, not today!"

The plane finally came to a stop at hanger 16, with Yani standing off to the side dressed from head to toe in a nice red and white Vallentino Garavanti outfit with shoes to match. Her lovely hair was blowing in her face as she boarded the private jet, smelling like a bed of roses with her expensive ass Viktor Rolf perfume sprayed all over her delicate looking body. Her beautiful light skinned complexion shined so bright in the midday sun. She looked more like a runway model than a cold-blooded killer. Especially with the way she walked onto the plane, it only signified what type of woman I had on my team.

She always walked with her head held high, a trait that was taught to her by her dear father, who had passed away ten years ago. Her father taught her and her twin brothers to always walk with their heads held high, due to them not having anything to be ashamed of, even if they were from Haitian decent. They still commanded respect from wherever they went.

"Well, hello, beautiful," I said to her as she strolled onboard.

She smiled at me and then kissed me on my right cheek as she kindly responded, "Hello to you too, my bruda."

I took her hand and then introduced her to Rhynyia. "Yani, I would like for you to meet my girlfriend, Rhynyia Sexy Redd Santiago, and of course you know who that clown ass nigga is sitting over there."

She smiled as she greeted Rhynyia for the first time. She then held out her hand. "It's finally nice to meet the woman who has Michael's heart and mind, along with his nose all turned upside down."

Rhynyia cut a gorgeous smile her way. "The pleasure is all mine, Yani.

They shook hands and then embraced each other with a gentle hug.

"Please be seated."

"Thank you, Michael. So, what's up?"

"Nothing much. Just business as usual, young lady," I uttered.

Maria brought out glasses of Chardonnay and passed them around.

Rhynyia had just reached for her glass as she pulled Maria close to her and whispered, "Let Miguel know that we can take off whenever he's ready."

"Yes, Princess, I will let him know." Maria walked towards the cock pit to inform Miguel of the news.

Yani slowly sipped from her glass and was positioning herself in the seat when she looked over at me and whispered, "Did I just hear her call Rhynyia Princess?"

"Yes, Yani, I'll explain it to you when we land in Orlando."

Yani then slid off her Gucci shades and stared at Rhynyia who was now sitting right up under me as if I was going to leave her. "When I boarded the plane, I didn't know for certain, at first I thought dat my eyes were playing tricks on me. But now dat I'm looking at you, you are her!"

"What are you rambling about now, Yani?" I asked her, trying to hold back from laughing.

"Michael, your girlfriend is Princess Rhynyia from dat small island outside of Puerto Rico!"

# CHAPTER 21
## THEIR DEMISE!

Poor Yani. She was sitting there looking as if she had seen a ghost. Rhynyia and myself were still laughing.

Rhynyia calmly replied, "Yes, that would be me, Yani, but please, that is only when I'm back home amongst my people. Right now, I'm on American soil, so please call me Rhynyia, or when I'm out dancing with those broads, you can call me Sexy Redd!"

They both smiled at one another, while Firstborn sat there sipping on his third glass of Chardonnay.

By the time we were back in the air amongst the clouds, it was seven in the evening. We would be back in Orlando within an hour, and I still hadn't come up with a plan on how we were going to rescue Sharon. So, while Firstborn and Yani sat across from Rhynyia and I, talking about how they disposed of Bernard, Rhynyia and myself began to put together a plan of attack for rescuing Sharon from the hands of Lieutenant Richards and his crooked ass partners.

"Once we get back to the house, Michael, I'll have all the Murder Queens get together, so we can put together a plan that should allow all of us to get Sharon out safe and sound."

"But we don't even know where they're holding her and her daughter."

Mister I Want To Have Some Money For Our Vacation stood up and shouted, "Nor do we have all the money that he's expecting to get for her safe return!"

"And why is that, Firstborn?" Rhynyia asked him.

He was silent for a brief second, then put a stupid ass look on his face. "Ah, you see what happened is, Michael and I—"

"Nah, playa, you took the money. I had nothing to do with it!" I shouted, looking away from Rhynyia before she even got started.

"Okay, you two, calm down. Michael, you know that money is never a problem with me. Whatever the price, we can pay it. We just have to make sure that whomever has her doesn't harm her." Rhynyia stood to her feet.

"Damn, now that's what I'm talking about. A sister that has her shit well put together."

"Whatever, Firstborn. Michael, chirp him back and let him know that we'll have his money and for him to allow you to speak to Sharon, so that we can make sure that she's still alive," Rhynyia recited.

"So, who is dis dat we are dealing wit?" Yani asked while seated, looking up at Rhynyia.

"I don't know. It seems as though Mister Michael here and I guess some of his friends have gotten themselves tangled up with some crooked ass cops."

"It wasn't that, Yani. Those two crooked cops that Firstborn and some of the girls took care of the other day had partners. And now the thirsty ass bastards want whatever money that was left behind."

Out of nowhere, Rhynyia sat back down and asked me, "So, Michael, how did they connect you to the demise of their partners in the first place?"

I looked over at Firstborn who was sitting there with a puzzled look on his face. Then I looked over at Yani, who was looking like, *'What are you looking at me for?'* I asked myself, *Damn, how did they know that I had something to do with their demise?*

# CHAPTER 22
### DON'T BE STUPID!

As everyone on that plane got quiet, I pondered over how in the hell my name came up in the first place. Somebody had to say something or maybe they were following those two cops. Whatever it was, the answer was right around the corner, and I wasn't too far away from finding it. It would be only a matter of time before we would meet up face to face with Lieutenant Richards and his gang of ruthless cops. The question that remained in the back of my head was were we all ready to meet up with what they had in store for us?

The plane was about to land once again, and this time we would all be getting off, only to come face to face with the enemy at hand. I still had to chirp Lieutenant Richards, so I decided that I would chirp him once we got back inside the limo. I just hoped and prayed that Sharon and her daughter were safe and sound, not to mention the unborn son that she was carrying for me as well.

Meanwhile, Mignon and Strawberry impatiently sat outside, waiting for Nicole and Entyce to emerge from the eating establishment. Strawberry nervously looked over at Mignon and said, "Damn, Mignon, what do you think is taking them so damn long in there?"

"Strawberry, how am I supposed to know? Hell, I'm sitting out here with your over-anxious ass!" Mignon replied to Strawberry as she was looking left and right, checking to see if anyone had noticed them parked out back behind the building.

"Fuck, this shit is taking way too long. I knew that I should've went inside. By now that fine ass brother would've been dead!" Strawberry yelled as she began rubbing her legs as if she had to take a needed piss.

"Well, if you feel like you could be doing whatever better than Entyce is, take your apple headed ass on in there and get this party started!"

Strawberry then took out her chrome plated four nickel and started looking over it as though she were really admiring the nice piece of steel she held in her hand. She then turned to Mignon, who was seated in the passenger seat, trying to hold on to what composure she had left. "Yeah, I think that I need to get in there and see what is taking them so fucking long."

Mignon was trying to ignore Strawberry when she replied, "Don't be stupid, Berry. You just can't go up in there and start shooting up the whole damn restaurant. Now put that damn gun away before someone sees us out here and think that we're about to rob the joint!"

"Damn, I feel like putting a hole in a nigga right now!" Strawberry put the gun between her throbbing legs.

"Just be patient my young friend, the time will present itself shortly. My girl Entyce knows exactly what she's doing."

Inside the restaurant, Nicole was just saying to her mother, "Okay, ma, listen. When I finish eating, if I feel up to it, I'll drive back to Orlando tonight, so I can spend some time with my favorite girl."

"I won't sit here and hold my breath, child. Whatever you decide to do, Nicole, just know that I love you."

"I love you, too, ma. Bye."

"Bye, Nicole." Her mother hung up the phone.

Nicole sat there for a second and then wiped away a single tear that had begun to snake down her beautiful face, not noticing the handsome man walking up on her, ready to end her precious life.

# CHAPTER 23
## HER LAST MEAL!

Nicole really loved her mother and yearned for her affection. She even wanted to be just like her, but knew that her mother would never approve of the notorious lifestyle she had grown accustomed to living, ever since she had moved out to become a stripper.

One minute after Nicole hung up the phone, a nice young, handsome, tall gentleman walked up to her table with a smile beaming over his face. His lips slowly moved as he asked, "Excuse me, ma'am, are you eating alone?"

Nicole lifted her head to see who the nice voice belonged to. She looked at how nice the young man was dressed. "Yes, I am. Why do you ask?"

"I was praying that you would say that so that I could ask you if I could join you."

Nicole hesitated for a minute as she thought of the man who had broken her heart only a few days ago. "Yes, I guess it won't kill me to have you sit down with me over dinner." Nicole didn't realize that death was actually knocking at her front door and she had just let him sit down with her. For her very last meal.

"Damn, this dumb naive chic, done let this smooth ass killer sit down with her silly ass," Entyce mumbled to herself as she was watching everything unfold. Entyce abruptly pulled out her Nextel phone and chirped the girls who were sitting outside waiting on her and Nicole. Her over excited voice came directly through Mignon's phone. "Yo, this bitch just let the damn mark sit down with her for dinner."

"She did what?" Mignon shouted into the phone as she chirped back.

"The damn dude who is here to kill her and I guess us too, is sitting right in front of her, showing off all of his gold teeth. "

"Okay, calm down, Entyce. Somehow get her attention and have her meet you in the restroom without causing the mark to feel like something is wrong!"

"Alright, let me see what I can do. It's real crowded in here. So, give me a few minutes."

"Please excuse me for being so rude. I should've introduced myself before I sat down here with you. I'm Rasheed." He then held his hand out for Nicole's.

She responded, "It's a pleasure to meet you, Rasheed. My name is Nicole." She placed her soft hand inside the large hand of Rasheed, AKA Death Certificate

"Nah, the pleasure is all mine to meet such a beautiful young lady as you are." Rasheed complimented her as a boyish smile ran across his face.

"Why thank you. You're not so bad looking yourself."

They continued their conversation when the young, beautiful waitress came back to the table with her food. "Excuse me, sir, would you like to order something as well?"

Rasheed was still smitten by Nicole's beauty to realize that their waitress was the elegant, sexy, tantalizing Entyce, standing there with the tray of food, staring at a wide-eyed Nicole.

# CHAPTER 24
## HEAD OVER HEELS!

Rasheed never bothered to even look at where or whom the sexy sounding voice came from, as he just uttered, "Yes, let me have what she's having, please."

"Yes, sir, right away," Entyce responded to Rasheed as she motioned for a stunned looking Nicole to meet her inside the ladies room.

As she hurriedly walked away, Nicole was still frozen in disbelief at the sight of Entyce.

It wasn't until Rasheed said something that snapped her back to reality. "Nicole, is everything okay?" he asked her, as his smile pierced her heart.

"Oh, yes, please forgive me. For a minute there I thought that I had seen someone from my past. Could you excuse me while I go to the ladies' room to freshen up?"

Rasheed stood up as a gentleman should do, when a young lady excused herself. "No problem, beautiful. I'll be here waiting on your return," he uttered as Nicole walked away blushing. Rasheed couldn't help but notice how nice Nicole's ass looked inside her black Dior jeans. He was still smiling as he mumbled to himself, "Damn, should I fuck this trick bitch first, and then kill her? Or should I just kill her and get on with my mission? It would be a whole lot different if the bitch wasn't so damn gorgeous."

With all of that brewing inside his head, there was something else prohibiting him from doing either one to

Nicole or her sisters in crime. When he took the job, he didn't realize just how cute the females he was hired to kill were. In all of the years of him being a hired killer, he had never let his inner feelings get involved with his mission at hand. Now he found himself with the job of dismissal of a beautiful Nubian princess. He felt as though if he was ever settled down, this female he was sent to kill would actually be what he needed in his crazy world.

In the mere minutes that she was gone, he debated calling Marquise so that he could let the man who hired him know that he was having second thoughts about carrying out his mission. He deliberated his actions for at least three minutes, and then he did the unthinkable. He retrieved his phone from his right pocket and thumbed through the list of numbers until he found the number of Marquise. Once he dialed the numbers, he sat back and waited for Marquise to answer.

"Hello?" The voice answered on the other line sounding all excited.

"This you, Marquise?"

"Yeah, nigga, did you put a bullet in that bitch's head yet?"

"Nah, man. I'm sitting right in front of her ass with mixed emotions." Rasheed replied.

Marquise snatched his phone down from his ear and stared at it for a minute before mumbling to himself, "Is this nigga crazy, or has he lost his damn mind?" He calmly placed the phone back up to his mouth and said, "Mixed muthafucking emotions! What in the hell are you talking about, Rasheed?" Marquise yelled back into the phone at a love-struck Rasheed.

"Man, I didn't know that this one was that damn fine. I think that I just might be feeling some type of way about this one," he muttered as though he was confused and head over heels in love already.

# CHAPTER 25
## RESTROOM!

Marquise was still somewhat alarmed and surprised by the remark Rasheed made in reference to Nicole. "Well let me remind you of what that pretty lil' female did, along with the other pretty lil' ones that she hangs out with. Not only did her and her girls kill my lil' brother, but they killed your punk ass cousin! Not only did they kill them, but it's the disfigured way in which they did their awful deed. First them lil' pretty ass bitches cut my brother's dick off and shoved it down your cousin's throat. Then took your cousin's dick and rammed it inside my brother's ass! Should I say more, my nigga?"

The entire time Marquise was talking, Rasheed was thinking of how fine Nicole looked as she walked away from the table.

Ten minutes earlier, as Nicole entered the rest room, she was reunited with her sisters Strawberry, Mignon and Entyce. She was just as surprised to see them as they were when she yelled out. "What in the hell?" She looked in the eyes of each one of her sisters for life.

"Girl, your dumb lil' ass is about to get whacked, and you don't even know it!" Mignon said as she was the first one to wrap her arms around Nicole's neck, who was still standing there with her mouth wide open.

"First of all, how did you hoes find me, and what in the hell are you talking about?"

"For starters, chick, you can never leave home without us finding you. Second of all, that handsome ass nigga you're sitting with, was sent down here from Jacksonville to kill all of us. His name is Rasheed AKA Death Certificate."

Nicole placed her hands over her still opened mouth. "What? How did he find me here in Daytona?"

A lil' short, fat white lady, weighing around a hundred and sixty-seven pounds with short, sandy blonde hair pushed herself into the restroom with her head held down, acting as if she really had to use the bathroom.

Strawberry was the first of the females to jump straight into action as she pulled out her loaded four nickel and shoved it right up under the lady's nose. She then placed an angry growl in her voice. "Take your short, fat, cheese biscuit-eating ass back out front and hold that shit, bitch. You shouldn't have been sitting your lil' fat ass down, eating up all the shrimp and crab legs in the first damn place!"

The lil' white lady then let out a lil' scream as Mignon grabbed her by her thick ass neck.

"Listen, we're having a family meeting right now. We don't mean to be rude, but now is not a good time!"

The frightened lady shook her head real fast as she stood there motionless.

Seconds later, the girls all started sniffing the air as if they were all smelling something real foul a midst inside the stale restroom air.

"What is that god awful smell?" Mignon asked as she looked over at Strawberry.

"Why are you looking at me? I don't know. I was just about to ask your lil' pretty ass the same thing!" Entyce then looked over at the short fat lady whose face had begun to turn beet red with fright, and shouted, "Man, this lil' short bitch done shitted on us!"

Strawberry then pulled back the trigger on her four nickel as she pinched her nose with her index finger and thumb.

The white lady whispered, "Excuse me, ladies, I seem to have broke wind."

"Broke wind? Bitch, your chubby ass did more than just break wind. I think that you need to check your damn britches. Heifer, you done shitted all on yourself and us," Strawberry said to the lady as they all pushed her stinking ass out of the restroom.

# CHAPTER 26
## DEADLY DEED!

Soon as the lady departed the restroom area, Mignon turned to Nicole. "Now back to you, Nicole! Just go back inside with your guest before he realizes that you've been gone too long. We'll figure something out."

Nicole looked at Mignon, still gagging. "What about Michael? Does he know I'm gone?"

"We haven't spoken to Michael all day. As far as we know, he's already in Puerto Rico. We hope, since the police came by the house earlier today looking for him."

"What? Why were they at the house?"

"That's a very good question. Now ask them two over there who sung like they were in a church choir on Sunday morning."

"Shut up, Strawberry!" Mignon shouted.

"Nah, what happened?"

"Nicole just get back inside. Once we get you out of here, I'll explain to you on the way home," Mignon uttered to an eager looking Nicole.

"Hey, Nicole."

"Yes, Strawberry?"

"Before you leave, grab me some of those hot ass cheese biscuits."

Nicole laughed as she went for the door. Just before walking out she turned back to Strawberry and said, "Chick, your ass is always wanting something hot off inside your mouth!"

The girls all shared a brief chuckle as Nicole hesitated before leaving the group that she had grown accustomed to. Entyce then shoved Strawberry out of the door, causing her to push Nicole as well.

"What?" Strawberry shouted as she turned around to Entyce. "I want some of those biscuits for real!"

"We know, Strawberry." Mignon replied.

Nicole stood by the door, motionless as if she didn't want to leave the girls' side. "Alright, where are you guys going to be?"

"Nicole, we're going to be right here with you, chick. Just keep your friend busy and we'll do the rest." Mignon muttered.

"Hey, stop acting like a scared lil' bitch and take your scary ass back in there with his ass before he starts worrying about where your scary ass went!"

"Damn, Strawberry, when did you grow them big ass balls of yours?" Nicole voiced.

Strawberry was ready, waiting to jump into action when time permitted for them to do the deadly deed.

"She's right, Nicole; we got this." Entyce voiced as she tugged Nicole by the arm.

Rasheed was still on the phone with Marquise as he noticed that Nicole hadn't made it back to the booth yet. He had just turned his head to look towards the restroom when he spotted Nicole walking back to the booth. He abruptly recited to Marquise, "Hey, listen, I'm gonna have to call you back." He then hung up the phone with Marquise in the background screaming.

Marquise looked at his watch and thought about jumping in his truck and driving down to Daytona himself, but quickly changed his mind as a customer walked into his rib shack, ready to place their order.

Nicole calmly sat back down while looking at Rasheed. "I hope I wasn't interrupting anything, was I?"

"Why, of course not beautiful. That was just my boss."

Nicole sat back down looking over her food. She had to quickly regain her composure to make it seem as if nothing was wrong.

# CHAPTER 27
## WHAT TO DO NEXT!

Nicole had to put on her best performance yet, not wanting Rasheed to know that she knew what his purpose for her and her friends were. The only thing wrong with her plan was the mere fact that being the type of person Rasheed was, he noticed everything around him. It all started when he noticed that his food hadn't arrived as of yet.

His keen sense of awareness told him that something was wrong. Why hadn't the waitress made it back? Just as he went to turn around, her lovely voice resonated through the nice smelling aroma of the food.

"Here you are, sir. Sorry that it took so long. Will there be anything else?" the waitress asked.

"No, ma'am. For a minute there I thought that you had forgot about me," Rasheed said to the waitress with a smile. That quickly changed, when he saw the elegant face of their waitress, who placed his food in front of him.

"No, sir, we just have a lot of people in here today, so we're a tad bit behind," Entyce replied as she turned to walk away. Once she got back to the kitchen area, she handed the real waitress a crisp hundred-dollar bill.

Strawberry shouted, "Hey, don't forget that bag of them cheese biscuits. Make sure them thangs good and hot, too!"

"Girl, you're a trip!" Entyce said as she cut a shy smile back in the direction of her good friend.

With the evening turning into night, Nicole and Rasheed sat there looking into each other's eyes. The only difference now was that Nicole knew why he was there, but Rasheed didn't know that the tables were turned on him. Not only was he staring in the sultry, sexy eyes of his adorable prey, but his prey was staring right back at him. To makes matter worse, she wasn't alone. She had all of her sisters there with her, ready to make their move.

Both finished their meal when Rasheed excused himself from the table so that he could utilize the restroom. "I'll be right back, ma."

Nicole sat back in her chair and took a deep breath of air as she watched Rasheed walk away. "Damn, and this nigga is bow-legged, too," she said to herself as she watched Rasheed walk all the way to the restroom. She then rolled her eyes and mumbled to herself again, "Why can't I find me someone like him to be all mine?" Then she thought of the one man her heart really belonged to.

Who was she fooling? The only man she wanted in her life was Michael Vallentino. So, as she sat there alone again, she thought of calling him and cursing him out for being with another female over the past weekend. But then she realized that he was probably in Puerto Rico by now with Rhynyia, so she would have to wait.

Minutes later, the tall, handsome brother was sitting down in front of her when the waitress handed Rasheed the check.

"Let me take care of this." Nicole snatched the check out of his hand.

"Nah, by all means, let me handle it. A woman should never have to pay for a man," Rasheed said as he went to pull out his credit card.

*Wow, and he's a perfect gentlemen*, she said to herself as she was smiling back at Rasheed.

"Man, I'm about tired of sitting here watching these two fall in love with each other. Has this bitch forgot that this nigga wants to kill her and us!" Strawberry said to Mignon with a disgusted look on her face.

"If you ask me, Strawberry, somebody seems like they might be a little bit jealous."

"Whatever. I'm here to do my job and then get the hell out of here. We've been here all damn day. Hell, we haven't even had a chance to enjoy the beach!"

"Strawberry, please. We'll be leaving here in a few minutes. There is no way that I'm letting any harm be done to one of my girls." Her phone began to vibrate in her pocket. "Damn, now who in the hell could this be?" Mignon uttered as she went to answer her phone.

"Who is it?" Strawberry asked as she kept an eye on Nicole and Rasheed.

Mignon then slowly looked back over at Strawberry before muttering. "Damn, girl, it's Michael."

They looked at each other with their mouths open wide, wondering what to do next.

# CHAPTER 28
## STILL ALIVE!

While walking towards the limo, I pulled out my cell phone and dialed Mignon's phone. It took several rings before she picked up, and when she did, it was nice to finally here her lovely voice.

"Hello?" She sounded sexy.

"Hey, what's going on with you and the crew?" A smile suddenly came across my face.

"Nothing, just handling some small business."

Before I could say another word, Sexy Redd confiscated the phone and yelled into it, "What up, girl?"

"Sexy Redd, is this you?" Mignon asked her with excitement in her voice.

"Chick, who else do you think it is? Hell yeah, it's me. I'm back!"

Mignon instantly put her hand up over her mouth and whispered to Strawberry, "Girl, it's Sexy Redd."

Strawberry looked back at Mignon and immediately mouthed, "What in the hell is she doing back home?"

"So, what's up, girl? Where is everybody?" Sexy Redd asked.

"I don't know. So far as the girls that stay with you and Mike are concerned, just say we're out handling some Murder Queens business."

"Okay, I fully understand what you're trying to tell me. Let me give the phone back to Michael. I'll see you guys when y'all get back to the house."

"So you're gonna just snatch the phone out of my hand like I wasn't even talking to her?"

"Here you go, baby. I'm so sorry," Sexy Redd uttered as she kissed me on my right cheek while handing the phone back to me.

"Mignon, like I was trying to ask you before we got rudely interrupted. Where is the rest of the crew?"

"They're here with me, Michael."

"Okay, listen. Something has come up, and I'm going to need you and the rest of the Murder Queens back at the house."

"So, you didn't go to Puerto Rico?"

"No, the police tried to stop me and my brother before the plane took off. So, we turned around."

"By the way, some detectives came by the house this morning after you and your brother left."

"Yeah, and I guess you and the girls were the ones who told them I was at the airport."

"Yes, Michael, we did."

"Not me, Mike!" Strawberry yelled in the background as I cut a smile over the phone.

"Shut up, girl!" Mignon growled at Strawberry.

"Damn, Mignon, what else did you all tell them, and who was it that came by?" I asked her as Firstborn pulled out of the parking garage, headed towards Metro West.

"We just told them that you were leaving out of town; that's it, nothing else."

"No problem, baby girl. Don't beat yourself up over nothing. It seems like those same cops that came by are the ones that we're going to have to get rid of."

"Why? What happened?"

"Remember the two cops that you guys framed last week?"

"Yeah. And before I forget, Mike, Sharon and her baby are missing. It's been all over the news."

"I know. They're the ones who have them."

"You mean those two cops that came by the house this morning are the ones who kidnapped her and her daughter?"

"Yes, that's why we turned back around. They told me that they want their money back in order for us to get Sharon and her daughter back."

"Okay, Mike. As soon as we handle this shit, we'll be on the way back home."

"I hope that you all are not out doing a show behind my back, Mignon."

"Mike, trust me when I tell you that we're not out doing a show."

"Alright. Call me when you ladies are on the way back home."

"Gotcha, Mike. Peace."

We hung up, but I could sense that they were into something way over their heads. Whatever it was, it wasn't any of my concern at that moment. My only concern was with knowing how Sharon and the kids were holding up and if they were even still alive.

# CHAPTER 29
## TENDER STEAK!

As Firstborn merged off of the turnpike, headed back home, all I could hear in my head was the serene voice of Sharon's mother when she asked me to save her daughter's life. Then there was the comment she made about already losing one daughter and couldn't bear losing another.

That baffled me. Sharon never ever mentioned having another sister. Could her and Rhynyia be sisters, and neither one of them even knew about it? They sure as hell looked like sisters. Even her mother favored Rhynyia more than she did. As I sat there looking out of my window, I just blew it off and made a mental note to one day ask Sharon about her sister that she never mentioned.

\*\*\*

It had been several hours since Sharon and her daughter had something to eat. Sharon sat on the edge of the bed wondering when they would eat again, thinking of how much longer they had to endure the harsh reality of being kidnapped.

She then stood up with her arms folded across her stomach, beginning to pace throughout the small room as she tried to cry once again. She was so mad and distraught that no tears would form inside the wells of her eyes. She was all cried out. She then slowly walked over to the blackened-out window, trying to see where her and her daughter might be. She was only disappointed once she realized that there was no way that she was going to look out of the darkened window, since it was smeared with the darkest of black paint that she had ever seen.

"Damn," she uttered as she once again began to pace the small cubicle she called a room, thinking of what was coming next.

Minutes later, she began hearing the sound of the keys coming through the door, once again, slowly turning inside the steel structure that kept her away from their freedom. Her small daughter, being frightened of the sound, vaulted back on the bed, terrified of who and what was coming from beyond the door.

The door slowly crept open, just far enough for the same frail white woman to emerge from behind it with another tray of food. The woman then placed the tray on the floor and started walking out of the room backwards; making sure that she kept her small, beady grey eyes glued on Sharon. This time, Sharon didn't mumble a word as the feeble looking woman closed the door and turned the key, making sure that her capture remained. Sharon hesitated at first, before she decided to see what the tray of food consisted of.

When she finally opened it, she was somewhat surprised to see two nice size juicy steaks, along with some mashed potatoes and once again, asparagus. She laughed to herself as she picked up a stalk of the green vegetable and said, "These have to be some asparagus eating ass crackers to keep feeding us this bullshit!"

As Breanna bit into the seasoned, tender steak, she looked up at her mother and asked her, "Mommy, when is Mister Michael coming to take us back home?"

Sharon looked back at her daughter and simply replied, "Soon, baby. Soon."

# CHAPTER 30
## VACATION!

By now, she had calculated that they had been held against their will for at least two days. By listening to the sounds in the background, she knew that they were nowhere near any possible civilization. Just how far away from people, she just didn't know.

With her and her daughter small bites of the food, she knew that she needed all the energy and strength possible for the plan that she was devising in her head to help them get away from their captures.

An hour later, a tall white man burst inside the room, weighing around two hundred and twenty pounds, standing about six foot four inches in height, with very dark brown eyes and sandy blonde hair. The very noticeable scar on the right side of his face triggered something inside her head, as she immediately put her head down so that she couldn't make eye contact with the very large man. For some odd reason, she felt as if she actually knew the man, or maybe she had seen him somewhere before. She just couldn't put her finger on it at the time.

"Listen closely. We're about to call your boyfriend, and you're going to tell him that you and your precious lil' daughter here are safe and sound. One false move and I'll kill both of you right here; do you understand me?" he barked at her.

Sharon frantically nodded, letting him know that she knew exactly what he was saying. She then sat still and waited as Lieutenant Richards hit the chirp button on his phone.

"Yeah, go ahead," I voiced as he came directly through my phone.

"You know who this is, correct?"

"Yes, sir. Where is Sharon?"

"She's right here. Where is my money?"

"I have it. Now, let me speak to her."

"Michael."

"Yes, Sharon, are you okay?"

"We're making it. Michael, what's going on? Why has this man kidnapped me and my daughter?"

"It seems as though something went down and these crooked cops want me to pay for it."

Right then, at that very same moment, she knew exactly where she knew the tall man from. The police station. It was Lieutenant Richards, the same man who she saw right before they received the check for her cousin's death. At first, she thought about slapping the shit out of his ass, then she thought of her daughter and what would happen if she put her hands on him. So, she calmed her nerves and did as she was told. She knew that it would only be a matter of time before she would have her revenge.

Just as he was pulling the phone away from her mouth, he uttered, "So, Mr. Vallentino, I've done my part, now where is my money?"

"Like I said, I have your money right here with me. When and where do we meet for the exchange?"

"I will hit you back on the hip in about two hours to arrange the drop off spot. Make sure you answer."

After we hung up, I looked out of the passenger window to see just how far away we were from the house. Firstborn had us on Interstate Four about to get off on the Universal

Studio exit. Once we got off the exit, it was only a few more minutes until we would be home.

I still hadn't heard back from Mignon and the girls, so I didn't know what was going on with them. I hadn't heard from Nicole or any of the other girls as of yet, either. To their knowledge I was already down in Puerto Rico, enjoying my little personal vacation, away from the Florida Hot Girls.

# CHAPTER 31
## NO-NO-NO!

Rhynyia was a tad bit joyless and couldn't wait to get out of the limo so that she could stretch out those nice, long caramel-colored legs. It had only been a few weeks she had been away, and now just looking at her made me want to have her extended over our bed, butt ass naked.

She happened to look over at me, gazing at her sheer elegance and beauty and said, "Hey, you. I know exactly what's on that freaky ass mind of yours. But not until we handle this business. We have seventy-two hours to rescue your baby mamma, then it's back in the air, headed back to Puerto Rico, Michael."

I put my head back in my palms and watched the way her words rolled off of her lips, when my manhood took control of my little predicament.

Before I knew it, she was placing her hand over my swollen manhood, saying, "Okay, Michael. When we get home, you have one hour inside this good ass Puerto Rican pussy. After that, we're going to be all about the business at hand."

"Enough said my Puerto Rican Princess," I recited, as a genuine smile ran across my face, elated that I was about to get to enjoy something I had been longing for since her untimely departure.

Ten minutes later, we were pulling up in the driveway of the house. There were too many cars inside the garage, so Firstborn had to park the limo outside of it beside the house.

I was rushing out of the limo with Rhynyia by the hand as I turned to him and said, "Hey, grab our luggage, please. I have something to take care of real quick!"

He just looked at Rhynyia and I as we both sprinted into the house. "Yeah, whatever, Baby Boy. Do you." He then took the bags out of the limo and then pulled a Black and Mild cigarette from his pants pocket and lit it.

Minutes later, Rhynyia and I were butt ass naked in our bedroom. At first, I laid her across the large bed and spread her legs just far enough for me to position myself just right so I could taste the sweet honey nectar that flowed from between her thighs. I positioned my head and then started sucking on her clit as she yelled out my name in Spanish.

"Miguel, Miguel, Miguel. Please don't stop, Papi. Eat my lil' fat-fat like you've been missing it for years!"

An hour later, she jumped into the shower as I laid there breathing all hard and shit, trying to catch my breath, while channel searching for something to watch on television. I had just stopped at Channel Eleven when I saw the caption flashing, *Breaking News!* I turned up the TV to hear the news reporter recite, "We're live here at the Red Lobster on A-1-A in Daytona Beach, Florida, where just about forty five minutes ago, there was a horrific shootout between several individuals at this very popular eatery. Right now, we don't know the actual number of casualties. All we know is that a group of females dressed in all black started firing at someone running out of the restaurant right behind us here. We have some small footage of the females who were all firing at one male assailant, who was seen moving very fast out of the establishment."

I immediately raised up in my bed to witness the footage when I noticed something familiar about the females shooting at the guy running out of the building. It was something about the way the females were wearing their hair that caught my attention. As I eased off the bed to get a better look, I threw the remote to the floor as I started screaming, "No-No-No, it's the damn Murder Queens!"

# CHAPTER 32
## THAT AWFUL DAY!

The girls fleetly climbed back into the stolen car that they borrowed, making sure that they were not being followed by any innocent bystanders. After checking their perimeter, the ladies immediately began checking over their bodies to make sure they were unscathed by any of the bullets fired back at them. During the melee, they didn't actually know how many times they had hit their target; all they cared about now was getting back to Orlando before all hell broke loose in beautiful Daytona Beach, Florida.

From the backseat, Nicole placed her hand over the front seat and yelled to Strawberry, who was driving somewhat recklessly back through traffic. "Here, chick! The next time you want some fucking hot ass cheese biscuits, get them your damn self. Now drive this bitch with some sense. I have to get back to the hotel and pick up my damn car and clothes!"

"Gee, that's the thanks I get for trying to save your punk ass? It's cool, though. We're heading that way, anyway!" Strawberry yelled back to a still shocked and surprised looking Nicole.

While Strawberry weaved in and out of traffic, and listened to all of the commotion from the ladies in the car, the police and medical vehicles flew past them, trying to get to the crime scene at Red Lobster.

Mignon turned around to Nicole and Entyce, who were still frantically checking over their bodies as well, trying to make sure that they hadn't took on any bullets. "Listen up. Nicole, give Entyce your car keys while you go inside and get the rest of your things. If it's a rental, we can just leave it here and come back later for it!"

"Hell nah. It's my fucking car that I just paid cash for today!"

"Oh shit, my bad, home girl. What kind of whip is it anyway?"

"Shut yo' mouth, chick. Yo' girl is pushing a brand-spanking-new, cream-colored four door Acura Legend!" Nicole replied as the entire carload of notorious females placed a smile on their faces.

"Damn, girl, where did you get that kind of money to buy you a nice whip like that?" Entyce asked as she sat beside Nicole with her mouth wide open.

"I know how to save money; that's how!"

"Okay. Entyce, please have her car ready for you guys to go. Once you ladies have everything, meet us back at the house. Strawberry and I will already be on the road, headed back home," Mignon voiced as she turned back around in her seat.

"So, do you think we killed him, Mignon?"

"I really can't say right now Nicole, but with the way his body was jerking every time one of those hollow points hit his ass. I would imagine so," Mignon replied while removing particles of her black attire.

Mignon was absolutely right about Death Certificate's body jerking from the hollow point bullets. She was referring to every time that one of those bullets pierced his vast body frame, his handsome face displayed the pain that was going through his body at the same time.

Not even while he served over in Desert Storm did he ever endure the type of pain that was being afflicted on him that awful day!

# CHAPTER 33
## RELOADING!

As the black Ford Mustang G.T. 5.0 pulled into the parking lot of the hotel, Nicole and Entyce jumped out of the car, ready to get out of Daytona before Entyce could yell, "Hey, Nicole! Where is your car?"

Strawberry was already spinning out of the parking lot, headed back to Orlando.

"It's right there. The cream-colored Acura. Just hit the panic button!" Nicole shouted as she dashed inside the hotel, fleetly trying to go obtain her belongings.

Entyce hit the panic button. The car lit up like a Christmas tree on Christmas morning. "Damn, her whip is clean." Entyce said with a smile. She hastily ran over to the car while pushing the unlock button on the key chain. As soon as she entered, she sat behind the steering wheel admiring the beauty and smell of the newly purchased automobile. While waiting on Nicole to arrive, she mumbled to herself, "Man, when I get back to Orlando, I have to get me one of these nice ass cars!" She then pushed down on the gas pedal so that she could hear the nice roaring sound of the engine.

Still mesmerized by the beauty of the car, she didn't see the nighttime security guard fleetly approaching. She continued to rev the engine and bounce her head to the beat of the very loud music that she was blasting from the high priced Boise Stereo System.

The lonely looking security guard, who had to feed a family of six kids and a wife off of his low-income salary, looked like a police officer as he nervously knocked on the driver side window of the car.

Entyce never heard the knock as she continued to bounce her head to Tupac's song *Hail Mary*. It wasn't until she saw his shadow in the background of the car that she knew he was even standing there knocking on the window. At first, she hesitated and thought, *Where in the hell is Nicole's slow ass? I'm about to do this damn cop, and her ass is still somewhere fucking around!*

Just as she went to pull out her black 9-millimeter from between her sweet-smelling vagina, Nicole was sprinting towards her car screaming to Entyce, "Entyce, no!"

Entyce then turned around to see Nicole running at full speed in her direction. As soon as she saw the expression on Nicole's face, she took her hand off of her loaded weapon and rolled the window down.

"Excuse me, ma'am. Could you please turn your music down?" the Security Guard asked Entyce, with a scared look on his face.

"Sorry, sir, I didn't realize how high I had it turned up," she replied to the officer, looking up at him.

Nicole then jumped inside her car, looking at Entyce as if she knew what she was about to do to the poor man. "Drive, girl. Get us out of here before you kill an innocent man."

"What took you so damn long?"

"Chick, I had to go back down to the front desk and get the rest of my money!"

"I thought that you had got held up or something; as long as you took."

"My bad, girl. I'm glad that I got out here before you put a big ass hole inside that poor guy's head!" Nicole said to Entyce, while taking the clip out of her gun and reloading another one.

# CHAPTER 34
## WHO DID IT?

With the nighttime security guard slowly walking away, Entyce looked over at Nicole and uttered, "Man, I'm sure as hell glad that you came out when you did. I was just about to put one of these hollow point rounds off inside the poor man's skull."

"Yeah, I'm glad that I did, too, because I would hate for the poor man's family to have to have dinner tonight without him being there," Nicole recited.

"Girl, when did you get this car again?"

"Chick, like I stated earlier, I paid for this car cash earlier today. when I was leaving you and the girls behind." Nicole rumbled through her purse as if she was looking for something.

"My bad, chick."

"Damn, I believe that nigga was in my room, before he found me inside Red Lobster."

"Why do you say that?"

"Because my room looked like somebody had been in there, and my damn purse was thrown over my bed as though someone was looking through it for something."

"Well, whatever it was he was looking for, I'm pretty sure by now his ass has found it." Entyce checked her appearance in the rearview mirror, trying not to laugh at her smart aleck comment.

"What I want to know is how that dude found me here in Daytona," Nicole muttered as they passed by the Krispy Kreme doughnut shop, headed for the interstate.

"They, he, or whomever else found us due to every time we go out of town for the weekend, them dumb ass broads that Mike be bringing be running their mouths, telling niggas where the fuck we live or where we're from!"

Nicole rolled her hair around her head. "You know you do have a point there, Entyce. Every time we go out of town, I catch one of them hoes running off at the mouth, telling people just too much information. When Mike comes back from Puerto Rico, I'm going to tell him about that shit."

"I hear you," Entyce replied, as she stopped at the light across from the mall on International Drive.

"Entyce, did you see that note I left on the counter this morning?"

"No, girl. Everything today has been a blur to me. It seems as though everything has been moving so damn fast."

"Damn, I left a note telling Michael that I was done with him and the group," Nicole recited as she rolled down her window and gazed upon the comely looking nighttime sky.

Entyce cut an evil grin at Nicole and uttered, "Girl, you know gotdamn well you're not leaving the group. So, I don't know why you even left a note like that. Stop fooling yourself, child. Everyone knows how in love you are with Mike and that dick of his."

"Whatever, Entyce. I'm really not sure if I want to be a part of this group anymore."

"Well, that's your ass. All I know is that after we saw the news about Sharon and her daughter being kidnapped, we thought that you had something to do with it."

"Wait a minute. Sharon has been kidnapped?" Nicole asked while displaying a sincere, shocked look on her precious face.

"Yes, girl, and we all thought that you had something to do with it since the girls said that you were acting a bit strange the last few days."

"So, let me get this shit straight. You dumb ass broads actually thought that I would kidnap Sharon's ass?"

"Hell yeah. Shit, how was we not to think that when, like the other girls said, you were acting as if you wanted the poor girl gone and out of his life!"

"Damn, I mean, I do love Michael and all, but not enough to take someone's life. Especially with the chick carrying his child."

"Like I said, we didn't know what to expect. We just all assumed that you did. So, while we were all at the house this morning, somebody from Jacksonville called Mignon's phone and told her that we all might be in danger."

"What?" Nicole asked as she turned to look at Entyce again.

"Yep, somebody from Black Magic called Mignon and told her about somebody named Marquise. Apparently, he hired this nigga Death Certificate to kill us for being the ones responsible for killing his baby brother and friend over the weekend. So, we really were concerned. First thinking that you had Sharon and then thinking that this cold-blooded murderer had you, Sharon and the baby!"

"How did the guy know that we were the ones who did it?"

# CHAPTER 35
## ALL OVER THE NEWS!

Entyce lethargically looked back at Nicole, taking her eyes off of the road briefly, as she said, "Your guess is as good as mine. I guess we'll find that out later. Right now, let's just concentrate on us getting back home without any problems."

Nicole sat there stunned for a brief minute, taking in what she had just heard, before she replied, "Okay, so tell me how y'all knew I was in Daytona?"

Entyce kept her head focused on the traffic. "I really don't won't to tell you this, but since you must know. Inside your purse is a tracking device that all of us have somewhere around us at all times."

"A what, Entyce?" Nicole asked as she pushed her seat back so that she could brace herself for what was about to come out of her friend's mouth next.

"Listen, Nicole, I didn't know about the device either, until that night those clowns tried to rob us back at the house. Remember the next day, when we all went shopping and met up with Mike's sister to discuss the Murder Queens?"

"Yes, okay. Now, please get to the point, Entyce."

"Somehow Mike knew about Jasmine and Do-Dirty. I guess he purchased some GPS tracking devices from that weird looking security guy."

"Talking about the one who hooked up the security system at the house, right?"

"Yes, Nicole, him. I guess after that day, Mike and ole sneaky ass Mignon somehow placed one somewhere on all of his top-notch females. You have to understand, Nicole, we're part of an elite group now. Not only are we a part of the Florida Hot Girls, but we're the damn females that keep everyone in this damn group safe. What would happen if we somehow got separated from one another?"

Nicole placed her head down and then uttered, "Damn, Entyce, what have we turned our lives into? One day we're dancers, and the next day we're some cold hearted killers!" Nicole had a tear stream down the right side of her face as she looked back in the direction of Entyce.

"You might as well suck those tears up, young lady. The sad thing about this life is that it didn't choose you, you chose it. So, dry them damn tears and accept what you have become. What we have to do now is take out that nigga named Marquise before he sends someone else after us."

As she continued to give the car more gas by pushing down on the accelerator, speeding down Interstate Four, neither of them saw the High Way Patrol officer perched in the cut, just waiting on someone to speed past him.

***

I was turning over in my bed, screaming at the television when Rhynyia stuck her head from behind the bathroom door.

"What is it, Michael? What's wrong now?"

"Those silly ass girls have really fucked up now!" I yelled as she walked out of the bathroom soaking wet from head to toe.

She was standing there in just as much shock and suspense as I was when she got a glance at the screen. "Oh my God, what happened?" she asked me as she turned around, with beads of water slowly dripping off of her splendid body.

"I don't know, Rhynyia, you tell me! You were on the phone with Mignon earlier. What did she say to you?"

"Michael, all she said to me was that they were out handling some Murder Queens business. That's it; I swear!"

"Well, apparently, you know more than I do, and I guess that's exactly what they were out doing. Handling some Murder Queen business. Now their dumb assess are all over the damn news!"

# CHAPTER 36
## EYVONNE RIDEOUT!

Rhynyia was drying off while I stepped out of bed and walked towards the window of the bedroom, staring out into the night time sky, silently praying for answers.

"Michael, what are you tripping about? You can't even see their faces, so how will they be able to  identify who they were?" she asked me as she walked up behind me, placing her right hand on my shoulder.

"Believe me, somebody got a good look at them before they put on those black outfits," I  replied, walking towards the bathroom.

"Whatever, Michael. One thing you can be assured of is when it comes to a plan, my girl Mignon carries it out to the T. Hell, she's probably on the highway right now bringing the girls back home."

"Yeah, whatever, Rhynyia. Just like I told my sister, I didn't want a group of girls going around killing people. Now it's like I have a whole team of cold-blooded killers. Next I'm gonna have a team of strippers for hire who go around murking people for money," I replied as I put on a pair of shorts so that I could walk down stairs to find me something to eat. I didn't know that the note Nicole wrote for me earlier was still waiting for the right person to read it.

"Michael, you're wrong about this group of women surrounding you. This group was not only your sister's idea, but it was something that I felt that we needed. You didn't seem to have a problem with it when them dudes tried to rob us that night!" she said to me as she followed.

"Yes, but look at what has transpired since we have them around. Don't get me wrong, they have gotten me out of some real tight situations in the last few weeks. But I didn't want them out there just killing random, innocent people."

"Michael, be for real. Do you think that those girls are out there just killing people for fun? Believe me, if they had to take someone out, they had to take him out for a good fucking reason!"

Firstborn walked out of the living room and voiced, "Hey, Mike, you might want to come check this out!"

I had just reached the bottom of the stairs and turned to walk into the living room to witness—

*"This is Eyvonne Rideout with Channel 11 Breaking News. I'm here still at the horrific crime scene at the Red Lobster, located off of Highway A-1-A. The police have now identified the murder victim as Rasheed Dontavious Marshall, also known as Death Certificate, from the Jacksonville area. All we know now is that he was involved in a fierce gun battle with a group of unidentified females. Paramedics say that the victim died in route to the hospital. All sixteen shots were located in the chest area of Mr. Marshall. Police believe that the individuals responsible for his untimely death were professional hit men. The only problem is that these were not men, they were professional hit women! The police say that they have one witness who believes that she met the women face to face in the restroom of the establishment, right before the shooting took place. Mr. Marshall was twenty six and had just finished his second tour of Desert Storm where he was a highly decorated solider. He leaves behind three children, along with his mother and father. We will have more information on this crime on the morning news. Please tune into channel eleven news for more up to date information. This has been Eyvonne Rideout for channel eleven news."*

# CHAPTER 37
## OH NO!

I couldn't believe what I was hearing. I turned to Rhynyia with a mindless stare and said, "Damn, didn't I just tell you that someone had to see them. Now they have a witness to what may cause them to link every damn killing back to those damn girls!"

"Michael, hold on. What if this person seen the wrong girls? We can't say that she even knows or seen the right females."

All I could do was just flop down in one of the chairs that were aligned inside the living room as Rhynyia came and sat down on the arm of the chair next to me, with all of her lovely ass perched beside my face.

"Michael, like I said, and like your sister told you a few weeks ago."

I densely turned my head up and looked up at her before I uttered, "Wait a minute. How do you know what my sister told me?"

"Michael, be for real. Don't you know?"

"Know what, Rhynyia?"

"Michael, your sister and I talk almost every day. She's not the only one who has something at stake here with the infamous Murder Queens," she said as she stood up to go get her something to drink from the kitchen.

I was walking right behind her, wanting to know how her and my sister were communicating every day and I only talked to her once every now and then. Hell, you're telling me that you know my sister on a more personnel level? Hell I didn't even know that you guys knew each other."

"Michael, I met your sister way before I met you. I'll explain everything to you when your head is a little less clouded," she said to me as she poured herself something to drink. "Do you want some?" she asked with a shy smile written over her face.

"No, thank you," I replied with a cold stare.

"Suit yourself. More for me," she said.

After pouring something to drink, we were walking back into the living room when the front door burst wide open. We turned, shocked to death at what we witnessed walking through the door. Mignon was dragging a wounded Strawberry into the house with blood flowing from an apparent gunshot to her upper body.

"Oh my God! Mignon, what in the hell happened?" Rhynyia screamed as we attempted to help Strawberry into the house.

Yani, who was standing on the stairs, immediately leaped into action as she shouted, "Take every ting off of da table right now. Lay dat girl down right here!"

Mignon looked up at me with her hair all tangled up and hanging down from her sweaty, blood dried face and said, "Mike, she didn't realize she was hit until we got halfway home. I'm sorry. Please don't let her die!"

I gently moved her hair and said, "No worries, Mignon. You did good. She's in good hands now. What happened, and where are the other girls?"

She then took a very deep breath and told me of how Death Certificate was hired by some guy named Marquise, and that he was sent to take them out. Then she told me about Nicole leaving the group, and that she was in Daytona when the guy Death Certificate found her and how he was going to kill her before killing them.

Mignon was telling me the story a mile a minute while Rhynyia was sluggishly walking out of the kitchen as if someone had shot her too. She held something like a letter in her hand. At first I was confused because I hadn't seen the letter or even knew about it as Rhynyia walked in with crocodile tears snaking down her face.

Mignon must've known what the letter said due to her looking at Rhynyia and then looking at me, before uttering, "Oh no, Michael, Rhynyia has the letter in her hand!"

"What letter?" I asked as I was attempting to make some sense out of everything.

# CHAPTER 38
## WHAT KIND OF MAN ARE YOU?

I was frozen stiff as if time had actually stopped. It hadn't stopped for everyone else in the house, but as far as I was concerned... It was over. "What letter?" I said as I looked at Mignon, who was dimly creeping away from me, looking at Rhynyia as if she was an apparition coming for her soul.

It wasn't until I turned around to see what had frightened her so, that caused her to want to get as far away from me as possible. Just as my black ass had turned around. *WAAAAAAP!*

Rhynyia had pulled back and unleashed a heavy right hand that hit me so damn hard that I fell back on my ass, causing me to think that I had lost half my teeth.

She then squatted on my chest and began yelling, "Michael, your black ass has been fucking this lil' tramp up in the muthafucking house that I bought with my father's fucking money? And you probably have been fucking her in the same damn bed that we sleep in!" She then quickly turned her head on a swivel, looking like the Exorcist and shouted, "Where is the bitch, Mignon?"

After she got off my chest, I rolled over rubbing my jaw, making sure that it wasn't dislocated, saying to myself, "What in the hell have I gotten myself into now?"

My conscience then stepped over me, looking down at me laying there on the floor, before pulling out one of his famous cigars. He then slid it inside his mouth, smiling, as he bit the end of it off before lighting it, and said, "Well, I guess Ms. Sexy Redd and myself will be the only ones headed back to beautiful Puerto Rico, playa."

As I laid there looking up at him, and still rubbing my jaw, Firstborn held out his hand and pulled me up off the floor, while saying, "Damn, baby brother. I guess you can't be a playa all of your young ass life!"

"Whatever. Make sure Yani takes care of Strawberry while I go upstairs and try to save what relationship I still have left with Rhynyia," I passively recited as I ran upstairs to our bedroom.

I knew she was inside the room because as soon as I got to the door, she turned up the stereo system, blasting the Ray Charles song, asking the question *What Kind of Man Are You?*

It stopped me dead in my tracks as if I was a deer stuck in the headlights when I heard the chorus:
*What kind of man are you?*
*Why do I love you so?*
*What kind of man are you?*
*When you love me no more?*
*What kind of man are you?*
*Why can't I let you go?"*
*I want to know, I want to know? About you?*
*What kind of man are you?*
*I just can't satisfy?*
*What kind of man are you?*
*No matter how I try...*

I couldn't move a muscle as my back fell hard up against the wall of the hallway. I knew I had hurt her in the past, but now I had really gone and did the unthinkable. I had cheated on her with one of the girls in the group, right dead smack in the house that she had purchased for us. I had also placed another child inside one of her closest friends.

As the song continued to play throughout the silent hallway, it sounded as if the female was singing directly to me, continuously asking me what kind of man was I. The answer was simple and written all of my face. What kind of man had the Florida Hot Girls turned me into?

# CHAPTER 39
## NO LICENSE!

I didn't know if I should've opened the door or just stayed outside of it. She was hurt, and I knew that she was still very angry at me. So, without even thinking things over, I lingeringly turned the doorknob. "Rhynyia, baby, please. Can I come in?"

She stood by the window, gazing out over the front lawn. "Hell, I can't stop you. You seem to want to do whatever your black ass wants anyway!" she said as she folded her arms across her stomach, walking away from the window, crying.

When she finally turned to face me, I could see that she was still crying, so I reached out for her, trying to pull her close to my body. At first, she tried to resist as she wildly took a swing at me. Her wild blow caught me dead smack in the chest, as I stood there and let her take out her frustration and anguish on me and my chest. Hell, I deserved it, so who was I to stop her.

***

As Entyce sped past the Deland-Sanford exit on Interstate Four, she nor Nicole realized that they were being followed by the Highway Patrol, until ten miles of him trailing them. Suddenly, without any warning, the blue lights hit the back window of the cream-colored Acura Legend.

"Oh shit!" Entyce yelled as Nicole quickly turned her head around to see what she was screaming about. "Turn your damn head around, chick!"

"Damn bitch, how fast were you going?" Nicole asked as she did what she was told to do.

"I have no idea, but I know his ass will surely tell me."

"You do have a license, right?" Nicole asked sounding nervous and scared.

"Hell nah," Entyce replied as she looked back over at Nicole, smiling. "But I do have this." Entyce cool and collectively slid out her weapon.

"No, Entyce, we have done enough killing for today." Nicole sighed and placed her weary head against her headrest.

"Girl, chill. I got this," Entyce said to Nicole as she cut a wicked grin over at her.

By now the officer had run the license plate and realized that the car had been recently purchased by a Nicole D. Jackson. The officer cautiously approached the car as Entyce rolled down the window. The young officer, who had just finished the Academy only a few months prior, stood around six foot two, weighing about two hundred pounds, with black hair and a very clean shaven face.

His voice was a very deep baritone as he leaned down into the car and said, "Good evening, ma'am. Do you realize how fast you were traveling?" The officer took a look inside the vehicle, making sure that there was no one else with them.

"No, sir, I'm sorry. My sister just purchased the car earlier today, and we were out just seeing how fast the car would go."

"Well, ma'am, you were traveling at a very high rate of speed. I clocked you doing at least a hundred and ten miles per hour. Can I have your license and registration please?"

Entyce looked at him and then over at Nicole before showing the man the license that she had told Nicole she didn't have.

"Excuse me, officer, it's my car and the only registration I have is this piece of paper that the dealership gave me earlier." Nicole said as she took a small piece of paper out of her glove compartment, and then handed it to the officer.

"No problem, ma'am, this will be fine." The officer took the paper and whatever Entyce had slid him, and fleetly walked back to his patrol car.

"What did you give him?"

"Don't worry, chick. Just sit tight; I got this!" Entyce smiled at what she had done.

# CHAPTER 40
### BACK HOME!

Entyce sat in her seat, cool and calm as could be while Nicole was still nervous and frightened half to death at what was about to happen next.

"So, what in the hell are you going to do when his ass comes back and tell your black ass to get out of the car with your damn hands up?"

"Nicole, girl, chill. I told your scary ass I got this! Now if he even makes his mouth say something like that, you better buckle that ass up and get ready for the wildest high-speed chase, ever!"

"What?" Nicole uttered as she looked over at Entyce.

"You heard me. Now, relax. I know just what to do," Entyce replied with that wicked smile still across her mischievous face.

"So, you're going to kill the poor man and drive off like no one is going to follow us! Man, this shit is fucking crazy!" Nicole recited as she slid out her weapon, checking it to make sure she had loaded it.

Ten minutes later, the officer was back at the window. "Since you guys just purchased the car, I'm only going to give you a warning. Next time I won't be so kind. So, please drive safe and have a nice evening, Ms. Thompson."

"Thank you, officer, and you do the same." Entyce then took her license from the officer and then looked over at Nicole who was praying that she didn't have to use her weapon. "See, chick, I told your punk ass that everything would be alright."

"Bitch, you told me that you didn't have any license. Who in the hell is Ms. Thompson?"

"I don't have any. This belongs to the waitress back at Red Lobster."

"Who?"

"The waitress back at the restaurant. I stole her license in case she snitched us out, I could find her."

"Shut up, Entyce. Just get us back home, 'cause this has been one fucked up ass day for me." Nicole placed her weapon back in her purse and placed her head back, trying to forget the day.

As Entyce merged back onto the highway, she felt the same as Nicole. If only they knew what lay ahead once they got back to the house, they just might have taken a different route.

The ride back to Orlando was nice and quiet. It wasn't the usual bumper to bumper traffic as it had been in the past. So, they made it back in just enough time for the fireworks to explode. When they reached the city limits of Orlando, Nicole kept her promise and had Entyce drive her to her mother's house so that she could see her for the first time since leaving home to go stay with the Florida Hot Girls.

# CHAPTER 41
## IS SHARON OKAY?

Back at the Vallentino house Yani was just finishing patching up the gunshot wound to Strawberry's arm. About thirty minutes after they had cleansed ole Berry up, she laid in her bed getting some needed rest, with Firstborn laying with her to make sure she was okay.

Yani then went to the guest room that she was sleeping in to wash up the blood that had gotten on her during the operation.

"Excuse me, Yani, can I speak with you for a minute or two please?" Rhynyia asked her as she eased into the room, cautiously.

"Yeah, my sister. Wat seems dab da problem?" Yani asked in her native tongue.

"Why do men have to cheat, Yani? Especially if you are so good to them?" Rhynyia asked as it looked as if she was still wiping away her tears.

"Listen, my young sister. Der will neber be ight answer for your question. Until you find de perfect man, all dat matters is dat Michael lubs you wit all he heart," she said as she stood there with her nice soft hips pressed up against the dresser.

"Damn that shit, Yani. It still doesn't answer the question of why he has to cheat!" Rhynyia said as she sat down on the bed, looking up at Yani while wiping away her tears that wouldn't stop flowing down her elegant cheeks.

"Girl, I don't know why you worry yo pretty self about who Michael sleeps wit, as long as yo heart and mind are pure."

"But, I don't won't my man putting his dick off in every woman that walks by, or comes to this damn group!"

While continuing to talk amongst themselves, I stayed in my room looking at myself in the mirror, asking myself why I couldn't keep my dick in my pants. Then I wouldn't be having all the problems I was having, like breaking hearts. The problem I was having now was that I had three beautiful women pregnant at the same time. While pondering over what I had done to those three women, my conscience stepped from behind me and stared at us in the mirror.

*You have no one to blame for your misfortune but yourself.*

*I know, and to think, I might just lose the one woman who has risked everything for me, and not to mention given me everything I've ever wanted in my complicated life.*

*Yeah, so you know what that means?*

I turned around and faced my inner self and asked him the million-dollar question. "What do I have to do?"

He blew out billows of smoke into the air before he bowed his head while staring at me with dark red eyes. *One day, you're gonna have to choose one of those beautiful ladies as the lady you want by your side.* He then placed his hand on my left shoulder, still holding his head down as I did.

"But which one do I choose?"

*That's simple, Michael. You have to choose the one that loves you the most, now answer your phone.*

"My phone is not ringing."

*Yes it is. It's your good friend Lieutenant Richards.* As soon as he said that my phone began to ring, and just like he had said, it was Lieutenant Richards.

"Hello."

"Mr. Vallentino."

"Yes."

"Are you ready for your instructions on where to bring my money?"

"Yes, is Sharon okay?"

# CHAPTER 42

## WHEN YOU GET BACK!

Lieutenant Richards hesitated for a brief minute, and then replied, "She's fine. Hold on while I get her for you." I could faintly hear him walking down what seemed like a long, quiet hallway. The footsteps stopped and I heard some keys to what must have been the door in which held her and Breanna captive. Just as soon as he opened the door of the room where they lay, I heard a very loud *Bam*, then a blatant thud as something or someone fell to the floor.

"Michael, is this you?" the voice asked, sounding hysterical.

"Yes, it's me. What just happened? Are you alright?"

"Yes! I just knocked his punk ass out!" she shouted as he began rumbling for the keys.

"You have to get out of there right now. Do you know where you are?" I asked as I ran down my hallway, trying to alert Firstborn and Yani.

"Damn, I can't find the keys."

"Sharon, listen, boo. Calm down, he just had them. Check his hands."

"Got' em."

"Cool, now get you and Breanna out of there, and tell me where you are."

"Okay, I'm looking for the quickest way out right now."

"No problem. Hang up and call me back when you are out of the building!"

"Okay!" she voiced as she clicked off.

Just as soon as I heard the phone go click, I was quickly yelling, "Yo, Firstborn, get the Denali! Sharon just knocked out Lieutenant Richards!"

He jumped out of bed with Strawberry, yelling, "What?"

"Sharon just knocked out Lieutenant Richards. She's trying to escape as we speak."

I ran to Yani's room where she and Rhynyia were still deep in conversation. "Yani, Sharon is trying to escape. It's time."

She sprung into action as she reached for her signature 9-millimeter, looking back at Rhynyia as if she was asking her was she okay.

I somberly looked over at Rhynyia who stared back at me with those beautiful brown eyes of hers. I asked her, "Bae, are you coming with us?"

She bluntly walked over to me, placing her weeping head on my left shoulder and whispered into my ear, "You go ahead and save your girl, Michael. If I'm here when you get back, we'll go from there. If not, consider me gone forever." She softly kissed me on my cheek, and then turned to walk back to our room.

At first, I just stood there, placing my head down into my chest, pondering over losing her and feeling sorry for myself. Seconds had passed when my conscience appeared before me and said, *You better go after her, before you lose her.* I quickly turned around and bolted out of the door into the hallway.

She had just bent the corner, heading into our bedroom when the door slammed dead smack in my face. I could hear her lock the door, as I shouted out in disgust. "Fuck!"

# CHAPTER 43
## NO GAS!

While trying to get downstairs, Mignon came out of her room dressed in an all-black outfit. I stood idle, gazing at how nice and fat her ass looked in her attire. "Damn, Mignon, you fitting them damn black stretch pants, aren't you?"

"Yeah, and it's too damn bad that you can't have any of what's in these stretch pants," she said as she ran towards the garage, smiling.

"Whatever, Mignon. Who said that I wanted to get inside them anyway?"

"Mike, that's what has your ass in so much trouble now. So, let's not get too far ahead of ourselves here. Try to focus on what's important. In other words, stop thinking with your lil' head and think with that big ass head of yours."

"Whatever." I had just got to the bottom of the stairs as I heard Strawberry from atop the staircase.

"Hold on, Mike, I know you guys are not going to leave me."

I turned back to witness her trying to ease down the stairs and said, "No, Berry. This is not your fight. And besides, there is no way that you're in any type of shape for what may lay ahead for us."

She fell against the wall that held her weak body up. "Mike, trust me, I'm good, and there is no way I can just lay

112

here while you guys are out there trying to save my lil' dawg Sharon."

"Seriously, baby girl, rest up. There will definitely be another day for you to go to battle. Right now is not the time." I could hear the horn blowing in the garage, letting me know they were ready to go. I dashed out to the garage and jumped into the backseat, next to Yani.

Firstborn turned his head back to me and said, "Mike, where are we going?"

"That's a good question. Let me call her and see if she has gotten out of there safe."

The phone rang one time before she answered. "Michael."

"Yes, Sharon, have you figured out where you are yet?"

"I have no idea. All I know is that I'm somewhere deep off inside some damn woods!" she shouted as I could hear her and Breanna running out of some kind of building.

"Sharon, listen, we have to have a location, so we can come rescue you." I then heard what sounded like her getting into a car which must've been Lieutenant Richards'.

"Okay, I'm inside one of their cars." She then turned the key in the ignition when she screamed. "Oh shit, someone is running towards the car!"

"Get out of there!" I could still hear the beeping sound of the car, and then I heard, *Blak, Blak, Blak!*

"Michael, someone's shooting at me!"

"I can hear that. Girl, you better drive that damn car like you stole it!" By now everyone inside the truck were listening to all of the commotion in the background. "Mignon, is there any way you can trace the phone that she's on? You know, track her by the GPS on the phone?"

"I'll try. Give me the number."

"It's 321-422-5464." Mignon then placed the number into the mobile tracking device and waited patiently for a response. "Sharon, get as far away as possible. In the meantime, we're trying to locate you."

"Fine, Michael. Do what you have to and make it fast!"

"Why, what's wrong now?"

"The battery on this damn phone is low, and there is no gas in this damn car," she angrily replied.

# CHAPTER 44
### THE OTHER MAN!

The GPS on our laptop had located where she was as Mignon turned around to me and said, "Michael, you're not going to believe where she's at!"

Sharon was in the background screaming, "Where am I, Mike?"

"Tell her she's somewhere outside of Sanford, Florida. Deep off in some swamps."

"Swamps?"

"Yes, swamps."

"Did you hear that, Sharon?"

"Yes."

I leaned forward and said, "Firstborn, get us on I-4 headed towards Sanford. I think that I just might now where she is!"

Sharon came back over the phone. "Mike, I have a small problem."

"What?"

"Someone is following me, and I know that I don't have enough gas to make it out of here!"

"Why do you say that?"

"Because the damn gas light just came on!"

\*\*\*

Nicole and Entyce had finally arrived at the house just as we had gotten onto I-4 headed to Sanford.

"Girl, I'm so damn happy to finally be getting back to this damn house," Entyce said to Nicole as they walked up to the front door. Nicole was somewhat skeptical about going in as Entyce turned to her and said, "Damn, chick, what's wrong with you? You act as if you don't want to come in."

"It's not that, it's just that there's something wrong. I can just feel it in my bones. And you and I both know that when I get to feeling like this, there's always trouble behind it."

"Girl, you're tripping. Come on. Let's get inside and find us something to eat."

"You are just as bad as ole Strawberry. Always wanting to put something in your damn mouth."

"Whatever. You must have forgot, I have my man upstairs for that; if his ass is even home," Entyce replied, referring to her now live in boyfriend, Resee.

"Whatever." Nicole sighed as she slowly walked in behind Entyce.

"What's that smell?" Entyce asked as entered the foyer.

"Hell, I don't know. I was just about to ask you the same thing. It smelt like that when you guys left earlier today?" Nicole asked as she gripped tighter to her purse that carried her piece.

"Not really. I wonder why it smells like blood."

"I have no idea, but I'm pretty sure we're about to find out," Nicole replied as they dimly walked upstairs.

"I hope the girls are okay," Entyce said as she looked over at Nicole.

"Yeah, me too."

"Why the long face, Nicole?"

"It's nothing; just thinking to myself."

"About?"

"How much fun Michael is having with his lovely Puerto Rican Princess," she replied as they reached to top of the staircase

They had just reached the door of my room when Rhynyia walked out with Nicole's letter in her hand. "He would have,

116

but it seems as though a bitch can't keep her hands off of what belongs to someone else!" Rhynyia growled as she went to draw back her fist, ready to strike.

"Oh shit!" Nicole yelled as she was caught off guard by Rhynyia's appearance.

"Bitch, I'm gonna teach your ass about fucking with what doesn't belong to you!"

Entyce had no time to react as she stood there witnessing what was about to go down.

# CHAPTER 45
## SPIRITS!

Before Rhynyia could put all her strength into her punch, Nicole wittily pulled out her four nickel and the next thing you heard was *Boom*!

One fatal round to the chest as the lonely victim fell to the floor. They stood there staring at the lifeless body sprawled. Their eyes grew as large as pancakes at how her body laid there motionless on the floor.

\*\*\*

As Firstborn bent a right, speeding down Kirkman Road, trying to get us to the interstate, all I could do was just sit back and hope that we got to Sharon before they did.

With me hoping and praying, Yani, slid her right hand over and placed it on top of my knee cap. "Remember, bruda, no worries, we got dis."

I cut a half smile back in her direction and replied, "Thank you for coming."

I had just turned back to stare out of my window when Firstborn alerted me with, "Mike, I think we have company!"

I quickly turned around to see three patrol cars tailing behind us. "Damn, well I guess we're about to be in for a very long night, my friends, so make sure your weapons are fully loaded."

Mignon was up in the front seat loading up two pump action rifles, while I was checking the magazine of my M-60 Grenade Launcher.

Firstborn turned back to me and uttered, "I love you, Baby Boy. If it's our time to go, always remember that!" He slowly turned around to see where his sentimental ass was driving.

"I love you too, but tonight is not the night that I feel like dying."

"I know that's right, Mike!" Mignon said to me as she continued loading weapons.

"Dats for damn sho, my bruda!" Yani chimed in as she was stuffing her pistols behind her back, looking like a real live gangster.

I took my eyes off her to see how far away the patrol cars were when my conscience appeared off to the left of the backseat. He had just lit another one of those expensive ass cigars when he looked at me and said, "Tonight is not the night for us to meet our untimely demise."

"How do you know that?" I asked as I turned completely around to face him, or myself.

"Because I have the Almighty up above on speed dial." He answered with a devilish grin.

"What?"

"And besides, our departure is years from now. Your destiny is to see every one of your kids and their kids reach maturity and beyond."

"Psst. Psst. Michael, who you talking to?" Yani asked me as she sat there with a confused look on her face.

"No one, Yani, no one." I went back to loading my 9-millimeter.

"I believe dat I know who you were talking to, but I be somewhat hesitated to say to you." I then lowered my head to retrieve another clip, when she said, "I believe dat you are talking to spirits, aren't you?"

I looked back at her and smiled before uttering, "No, Yani, it's myself. Just myself."

"Wat eber, my bruda. I know when this happens—"

Mignon yelled, "Michael, we sure as hell have company now! Look!" She pointed to the police helicopter flying high above us in the dark of the night. "Damn, well I guess we're going out in a blaze of smoke!" Mignon closed her eyes as she began to pray, while Firstborn got off at the Sanford exit and then made a left under the under pass. "Her location is two miles up the road and then make a right turn on Hatcher Creek Road," Mignon yelled as she continued monitoring the lap top, pointing up ahead.

# CHAPTER 46
## NO ONE LEFT BEHIND!

We lost the cops that were tailing us momentarily, but I could still sense their presence somewhere close behind us. All that mattered to me now was us reaching Sharon and her daughter in time. As Firstborn made a right turn onto Hatcher Creek Road, all we could see were woods and shallow swamps surrounding us.

"Hey, man, make sure you stay on this small ass dirt road! Looks like if you veer off to the side, we might be alligator bait."

"I see," Firstborn muttered, as he stayed focused on the road up ahead.

"Where is her location at now, Mignon?"

"Mike, we have a problem."

"What now, Mignon? Damn!"

"This damn thing has lost her signal."

"What? How did we lose the signal?"

"I have no earthly idea. Maybe it's due to these fucking swamps, Michael!" She was becoming agitated.

Then, I heard sirens in the distance as we traveled farther and farther into the swamps, the patrol cars were close behind us. I knew then that we were about to be in the fight of our short-lived lives. The patrol cars that had been following us earlier were now right behind us.

"Oh shit, Mike, look!" Mignon yelled.

I swiftly turned around from looking at the patrol cars behind us to witness someone standing right in the middle of the dirt country road. "Hold up. Slow down, Firstborn. What is it?"

The truck began to slow down so we could all see what was in the middle of the dirt road.

"Oh my goodness, Mike, it looks like the same police officer who came by the house earlier this morning. What is he standing over?"

The truck was barely moving as we all sat there dismayed to see Lieutenant Richards with a half-naked Sharon on the hard gravel road, holding her baby, screaming for him not to shoot her.

"Stop the truck," I shouted as I went to get out of the truck. Mignon tried to refrain me by grabbing my arm, but it was too late. I was already halfway out of the truck, and with all the anger and emotion that I had bottled up in me, it wouldn't have stopped me anyway. I was hell bent on saving her life, no matter if it meant me losing mine. "Alright, Lieutenant Richards, we have your fucking money. Just let her and the child go!"

He was standing over Sharon with blood all over his white shirt and dirt smeared over his JC Penny suit pants, his police issued revolver pointed down at the head of Sharon while she lay there weeping and sobbing frantically. "You know it's a damn shame that this had to end like this, Mr. Vallentino! All I wanted was my money, and we could have been friends. But no, your pretty ass bitch here had to go and break my nose with that damn dinner tray, not to mention her running over my mother back at the building, snapping her neck instantly," he said as he was dripping blood and sweat.

"Whatever. That bitch deserved to get ran over. Maybe next time she won't keep feeding a bitch asparagus!" Sharon shouted as she lay in pain.

"Asparagus?"

"Yeah, baby, that's what they kept feeding us!"

"Shut up, bitch!" He then slapped Sharon.

She yelled out in pain and anguish.

"Hey, I'm sorry that she messed up your pretty face and killed your mother. All we want is her and the baby. You can get your money and still be able to let us all go without any problems. I'll even pay to have your face fixed up along with the burial of your mother! What do you say about that?" I recited as I looked back into the faces of the individuals that were assembled to help me eradicate the dire situation.

"Yes, that would be mighty white of you and your friends. But my friends and I seem to have one small problem with that," he replied.

"And what's that?"

"In order to make sure that you get away with the perfect crime, you must not leave anyone behind to tell what really happened."

# CHAPTER 47
## SPLENDID LOOKING!

The bugs and insects had begun to suck the blood off Lieutenant Richards' face. The bites and stings that he was taking began to become very painful to his face as he reached down and ripped off a part of her blouse, revealing her nice thighs and a portion of her nice rounded ass, and started rubbing and fanning away the insects, with her laying there trying to keep the bugs away from her and her child. "You know, I almost made love to your beautiful Nubian Princess here, but you got here just a few minutes early," he yelled to me.

I stood there almost in tears, seeing her battered. "If your white, red neck ass would have laid one hand on her, I would have haunted you and your entire family down and killed them one by one!"

He was broken for a minute due to the way the blood was oozing down his face. I knew then that it would only be a matter of time before he would succumb to his open facial wounds. In the lights of my truck and his car, he continuously tried to fan away the bugs that were feasting on his blood and injuries. Sharon had caught him twice across his face— one blow breaking his nose, the other one breaking his right orbital bone under his right eye. She had really done a job on the old red neck bastard.

"Mike, we have company." Firstborn stepped up next to me, brandishing his weapon inside his slacks.

I abruptly turned to see the rest of his crooked partners pulling up behind us, stepping out of their patrol cars, demanding that everyone get out with their hands up.

"Please don't try anything stupid and no one will get hurt. I'm trying to get to the bank and then home to my family before this afternoon," one of the officers said as he darkly approached the truck.

"Mike, that's the other officer that came to the house this morning," Mignon whispered to me.

"Yeah, it looks like the one who was with Lieutenant Richards at the airport."

"Okay, since we all know each other. Get down on your knees and place your hands behind your heads."

"Hey, John, check the truck for the money!" Lieutenant Richards yelled over to his partner while he had all of us on the ground.

His partner then went through the truck. Once he found the black duffel bag, he stuck his head out and shouted, "Hey, Lieutenant! It looks like it's all here!"

"Okay, we did our part. Now can you please let her go?" I screamed.

"I might as well, since you all are about to die together!" Lieutenant Richards yelled as he picked up a small fraction of Sharon's limp body up off the ground and drug her across the hard rock and gravel of the narrow dirt road.

Tears wouldn't stop flowing as she screamed in agonizing pain as the gravel and rock tore away at her delicate, pure, splendid-looking skin.

# CHAPTER 48
## CYNTHIA VALLENTINO

I couldn't begin to imagine how painful it must have been for Sharon as he dragged her across the road in the way he did. She fell breathlessly in front of me with half of her breast hanging from her ripped bra, along with half of her beautiful pussy showing from where he had ripped her blouse. As she lay there still holding tightly to Breanna, who was covering up whatever else wasn't showing, she dimly looked up at me with snot and tears covering her beautiful face and uttered, "I'm so sorry, Michael. Thanks for coming to my rescue."

I was at a loss for words at that very moment. Struck with grief amid sorrow, I sluggishly turned to my brother, Yani and Mignon in thought. *Is this really the end?* I turned back to Sharon and whispered, "It's all good, baby. We're going to get out of here, somehow, some kind of way!"

Just as I had mumbled those words, I could hear Lieutenant Richards and his dysfunctional crew of officers talking amongst themselves. Then I heard them begin to lock and load their individual weapons. But just as the first weapon went to sing in the nighttime air, you wouldn't believe who came out of nowhere, blasting on them fools.

It was the one Murder Queen who finally decided to show up at the party. My damn sister. "Murder Queens on deck, Baby Boy!" she shouted as she started firing off her semi-automatic rifle.

We all were able to low-crawl back inside the truck and retrieve our weapons. There were rounds flying over our heads.

I quickly placed Sharon in the backseat as I whispered to Breanna, "Lay down with your mommy."

"Yes, sir," she replied, sounding a bit frightful.

When I stepped outside my truck to return fire, I looked behind us to see where the officers were.

"There's no need to worry about them, my brother. Them fools were dead before they even knew what hit their ass," Cynthia Vallentino uttered as she stepped over the one officer who had stated that he was trying to get to the bank and home before the midday.

"I guess his plans got interrupted," I voiced as I spat on his forehead, then joined my brother who was standing tall, firing off his 12-gauge pump shotgun, letting them fools have it.

Mignon's sexy ass was kneeled to the right of me, firing her tech nine semi-automatic weapon with her fat ass kitty cat protruding from her tight black spandex pants. With the way her kitty was all compressed in her pants, there was no way that she could've been wearing any panties. My eyes were glued to her fat, mouth-watering pussy.

My conscience stepped from behind the crossfire and bushes and uttered, "Alright, dumb ass nigga, you over there looking at how nice that pretty pussy of hers looks while your ass needs to be firing back at them crackers, before you and I be laying butt naked off inside Coney Brothers Funeral Home!"

I quickly snapped out of it and replied, "Yeah, you're absolutely right. What in the hell was I thinking about?" I then gathered myself and started popping off rounds from my Grenade Launcher, firing at everything moving.

# CHAPTER 49
## MEDICAL ATTENTION!

The gun battle was fierce, tense and of course very violent as round after round continued flying over our heads. We didn't know if we had actually hit anyone as we continued firing, hoping that it would all end soon.

It wasn't until I inserted one of my grenades and fired exactly where Lieutenant Richards was standing. After the smoke cleared, I heard someone screaming, "Paul, I think Roman is down!"

"Fuck him!" Lieutenant Richards yelled back to his partner John.

"That black son of a bitch, just shot at us with a Grenade Launcher! Call in back up!" His partner low-crawled over to where Lieutenant Richards was hiding, due to the array of gunfire being shot at his ass. He was shaking and looked like he had tears flowing down his alarmed face as he shouted, "Listen here you sick bastard, if we call in back up, the whole entire department will know what in the hell we were up to!"

Lieutenant Richards looked back at his partner with the blood and sweat pouring down his face, the color of dark beat red. "I'm not talking about the damn department, you fucking dumb ass city cop. I'm talking about our Klan brothers!"

"Oh shit, I didn't think about them!" John replied as he tried to wipe away the saliva that Lieutenant Richards had spewed on him while talking and wiping the blood out of his one good eye.

"Dahhhhh!" Lieutenant Richards said to his partner, with half of his face gone.

"Listen up, Richards!" I yelled across to them as the rounds stopped flying over our heads. "We can all walk away from this gun battle, unscathed. All you have to do is let us go."

He then shouted back to me, "Right! You must think that I'm one of the dumbest rednecks you have ever met. Nah, we're going to finish what we have here tonight. In just a matter of time, these swamps are going to be infested with some of the worst Klansmen your black ass has ever seen!"

My brother looked over at me with that look of fright and fear. "Man, there is no telling how many of them damn crackers will be headed this way! What do we do now?"

"We finish it, right now, right here! Before any of those tobacco chewing son of bitches get here!"

We all stood to our feet, firing round after round into them shallow swamp infested woods. Within a few minutes we figured that the gun battle was over as we jumped back inside the truck, my sister in her car.

My brother threw the truck in reverse, and we drove all the way out of the woods with him looking over his shoulder.

"Hey, man, slow down, you don't want to hit Cynthia!"

"Man, if she knows like I know, she better be pushing that damn car like she's in a damn hurry to see that lil' short ass nigga in Madison!"

"Who, Yetta?"

"Hell, I guess so; I don't know his damn name!" my brother yelled as he continued maneuvering my truck through the swamps, trying to get us out before backup got there.

"Man, you talking about Will's lil' brother," I replied as a smile crept along my face.

"Yeah, that lil' short ass nigga." He laughed as we both just smiled at one another.

As soon as we got back onto the road, he whipped the truck around and into drive and headed towards the highway. Once we got onto I-4 we looked over each other's body to make sure that no one had any gunshot wounds.

Our sister followed closely behind us, and Mignon rode shotgun with her. Sharon, who was badly bruised and shaken, was laying in the backseat with deep abrasions all over her beautiful body.

As I looked over her, I knew that she would need some immediate medical attention. That's when I shouted out to him, "Firstborn, get us to the nearest hospital!"

"Say no more, Baby Boy!" He turned back, winked and fleetly sped down the highway, headed to the hospital.

# CHAPTER 50
## AT THE HOSPITAL!

Sharon was exhausted just as much as she was beaten and battered. But what mattered most was the fact that she was alive and safe, now that her and Breanna had been rescued. She looked so innocent and serene, with her head turned to the right, nestled inside Yani's lap. I had to actually catch myself before I began to shed a tear for her when I slowly turned my head back to the front.

Firstborn had just merged onto I-4 and then pushed the pedal to the medal as the high powered Denali picked up speed. After he had a clear path in the fast lane of the highway, he looked over at me and said, "Don't worry, bro, I'll have her at the hospital in a few minutes."

I turned to look at him and uttered, "Yeah, I see that, especially with the way you're driving my damn truck. I'm sure we'll be there, or in somebody's jail by mid-morning."

"Shut up, man. Just lay your head back and take a load off of your feet."

"That would be nice, but with what we all just went through back there, that will be impossible. I'm pretty sure we haven't seen the last of them crooked ass cops."

"So, you don't think that there all dead?" he asked as he sped by the slow moving traffic in the left lane.

"Nah, but like I said, we'll all know something real soon," I replied as I stared out of the passenger window, pondering on our immediate future.

"Michael, what about her daughter?" Yani asked from the backseat.

I quickly turned around to see the still frightened Breanna just sitting there looking at me and then her mother, who seemed as if she was in a coma. "I'm about to call your grandmother so that she can meet us at the hospital, okay?"

"Yes, sir."

I then stretched my arms out to her so that she could come sit in my lap. I guess she could sense my sincere affection for her as she dully climbed over the seat and sat up front with me. I then began to thumb through my phone until I reached the number.

Her phone rang one time. "Michael, please tell me that you've found my daughter!"

"Yes, ma'am, we have her."

"Thank God," she said. I could her the relief in her bewildered voice.

"She has been through a lot, along with losing quite a bit of blood. We're on the way to the hospital with her and Breanna. It would probably be best that you meet us there so that you can get Bre."

"What hospital are you taking them to?

"Orlando Regional, ma'am."

"Okay, I'll be there in thirty minutes."

I hung up the phone just in time to see Firstborn passing by the Eatonville exit. It would only be a matter of time now that we would be at the hospital. "How is she doing, Yani?" I asked as I turned back to check, when at that very moment, I realized that Sharon had seen Yani's face in the picture when she took a look when the detective was at her house, trying to find her missing uncle. "Oh shit, Yani."

"What, my bruda?" she answered with a quizzical look on her face.

Sharon seemed to be still passed out as I whispered to Yani, "Make sure that she doesn't get a good look at your face!"

"What?"

"Yani, she cannot see your face! I'll explain it to you at the hospital."

# CHAPTER 51
## SPEEDING AMBULANCE!

As Firstborn pulled up at the emergency room entrance, I was about to receive the shock of my natural born life when the ambulance would bring her lifeless body to the same hospital that I had Sharon at. My once pristine black Denali came to a halt as I jumped out screaming for a doctor, when a few of the orderlies and one nurse rushed out of the emergency room entrance.

"Sir, you can't park here, we have an ambulance in route with a victim who has been shot in her chest!" the nurse shouted.

"Okay, and I have my girlfriend here, who needs immediate attention as well!" I shouted back.

"What happened to her, sir?" she asked as I stood there with Sharon's blood smeared all over my shirt.

"She was kidnapped!" I imprudently replied.

"Oh no, it's the young lady that was on the news earlier today!" She immediately knew who Sharon was and had the medical team leap into action.

Just as they placed her on the gurney, Sharon came to and reached for my hand. "Michael, please don't leave me. I love you," was all she said as they immediately rolled her down the hallway.

Bre, in Mignon's arms, cried, "I want my mommy!"

Mignon then carried her to the waiting area as the rest of my soldiers followed closely behind her. The people who were seated in the waiting area began to move around and make room for us, due to the way we all looked and smelled upon arrival.

My brother stood by the water fountain with dirt and grease all over his faded jeans, with his t-shirt covered with droplets of someone's blood on it. Mignon was standing by the soda machine with her black spandex pants covered in dirt, grit and grime from the road. Not to mention the constant smell of gun powder that seemed to resonate throughout the waiting room area. Yani had blood all over her pants from where she had Sharon's head lying in her lap, with her long, beautiful hair covering up her face, so that Sharon wouldn't recognize her if she would have woken up and saw her. I was standing by the front door with my slacks covered in dirt from being on the ground, with my two-thousand-dollar silk shirt being ruined by the soiled pants that Bre had on.

"You did good, Baby Boy. You did good," my sister voiced as she walked past me into the waiting room last.

"Thank you, and thanks for having our back."

"Don't mention it," she replied.

"Sir, I'm not going to ask you again. We need you to move your vehicle. The ambulance is in route with a badly injured young lady!"

"My bad," I replied as I went to move my vehicle, forgetting what she had told me only minutes ago. "Damn, I guess someone else had it worse than we did," I mumbled to myself as I ran towards my bullet riddled truck.

I didn't want to park too far away from the entrance, so I just moved the truck over into an empty doctor's parking space, not caring what anyone had to say about it.

Just as I closed my door and began to walk around the back, my conscience appeared out of the blue. "I told you that you would have to make a decision fast!"

"Make a decision about what?"

"The one woman that you wanted in your complicated life!"

"What?"

He then moved out of my way and pointed in the direction of the speeding ambulance that was making a bee line for the hospital emergency room exit.

I looked back at him and asked, "What are you talking about?"

"You didn't want to make the decision, so I made it for you."

# CHAPTER 52

## CARRYING YOUR SON!

We were just standing there as the ambulance wheeled into the emergency room entrance with me not even realizing what was happening. That's when he gloomily looked over at me, placing his hand on my shoulder, saying, "Look who they just brought in."

What seemed like a dream then became my worst nightmare as I darkly crept up to the ambulance rear door to see Entyce and Strawberry standing with Reese all crying and sobbing hysterically. "What the fuck?" I yelled, gazing down at who they were bringing out of the ambulance.

Reese held onto Entyce who acted as if she was about to fall to the ground in shock. That's when I shouted out to Strawberry, "Hey, Strawberry, please tell me what in the hell happened!"

All she could do was just look back at me while holding her head down, still standing there weeping like it was me on the damn gurney. She couldn't answer me, nor did it even seem like she heard me, as she stood there weeping her eyes out as if she was at someone's funeral.

The paramedics had her on the gurney wrapped up and it didn't look too good for her. As they were rolling her away, I was trying to reach out for her hand when her arm fell lifelessly off of the gurney, seeming as if she had taken her last breath of air.

That's when I heard the doctor yell, "I think we just lost her!"

I could faintly hear another passive voice behind me, but I couldn't turn around, I was so caught up with the female on the gurney to even look at another person. I was living my worst nightmare as I stood there in a frenzy. In all of my years of being on this earth, I just couldn't believe that I had just lost the woman of my dreams, and there was nothing that I could do to try and save her. I knew it had to be her because she had the jacket on when we stepped off of her father's private jet. I was baffled as to what had transpired.

Had she taken her own life because of my infidelity, or had she been murdered? The questions were all there, there were just not any answers. I couldn't bare to walk into the hospital to let the people who looked up to me the most see my like this, so I eased behind one of the concrete pillars and began to weep uncontrollably.

It wasn't until my conscience emerged around the corner of the building and said, "I should leave you to yourself so that you can drown in your own fucking sorry ass sorrows. But no, let me lay this one on your selfish, ungrateful black ass! The bitch was caring your son as well!"

My whole entire world meant nothing to me. I had let her down. I wasn't there for her and my unborn child when she needed me the most. The warning signs were right there in front of me, but I didn't take heed to them. I couldn't start to fathom how I had ever took her love for granted, now I was left with calling her father to let him know the awful news. His first-born child was dead!

First, I had to think of how I would tell him and then prepare myself and the others for the aftermath of what was going to take place next. I knew that he wouldn't take the news sitting down and there was probably a good chance of him wanting to take me and my family to war, since I was the one responsible for the safety of his daughter. Pierre Santiago would do what he did best, which was retaliate for letting his daughter lose her cherished life. He would turn every stone over until he found me and killed everything I ever loved. Which meant he would kill my entire blood line. My entire lineage of immediate family members, my children, their children and their children's children. It would continue until he was satisfied with my family be destroyed.

I could only imagine how he would feel. First it was his only son being murdered in cold blood, now it was his oldest daughter being killed on American soil.

As I walked back into the hospital, trying to find the room where they had taken her, I could still hear a faint voice calling out to me, but I wouldn't stop; I had to be by her side. Even in death I had to be near her. For some strange reason, I thought that if I stayed by her side and prayed to Yahweh up above, He might just bring her back amongst the living. Then and only then I could show him and her how much I really loved her.

After minutes of me searching for where she lay, I stood outside the operating room, watching as the doctors and nurses attempted to revive her. It wasn't until one of the nurses came outside and said, "Sir, we're going to have to ask you to please go back out to the waiting area. We will find you, if anything changes with her situation."

"Ma'am, I'm her only family while she's on our soil. I have to be here for her," I said to the short, petite nurse, who was wildly trying to usher me away from the operating room window.

The nurse stood around five feet even and probably weighed no more than a hundred pounds, soaking wet. She seemed to be of Asian decent, so it was very difficult for me to understand her as I stood there arguing with her about me staying there until I heard something about her.

Moments later is when the hospital security guards came and took my black ass back to somewhere private, away from where the others were seated. That's when I fell down on my knees and started praying loudly. As doctors and nurses ran back and forth, and with me kneeling, crying and praying, I still hadn't acknowledged the voice that kept calling out my name.

"Michael, Michael!" in the distance the voice sounded.

I just couldn't let the people I loved the most see me caring on the way I was, so I folded my arms across my knees so that I could support my head on them.

As I sat there with my head down, weeping like a grown ass baby, I thought that I heard one of the nurses say to one of the other nurses, "The patient's mother has just arrived, we're going to have to let one of the girls who came in with her explain to her what happened because we surely can't let that grown ass baby tell her!"

"What? Her mother?" I said to myself as I held my head up, frantically looking around for answers. "Wait a minute. Rhynyia said that she never found her mother." I sat there dismayed and confused, when the touch of her hand against my weary forehead and the sound of her radiant sounding voice, led me to believe that she had passed on, and was now an angel sent back to let me know that she was in heaven. That's when I slowly raised my head up to see a bright light shining on the face of the beautiful…

# CHAPTER 53
## NOT OVER!

Rhynyia *Sexy Redd* Santiago. I could barely see her elegant face as the light damn near blinded me. Her luscious lips were moving, but I couldn't hear her as I sat there staring at her as if she was an angel. It wasn't until she had to actually shake me when I heard her say, "Michael, I'm so sorry, baby! It was all an awful accident!"

"What happened? Is it really you?"

She smiled and then shed a tear. "Boy, what are you talking about?"

"I thought that it was you on the stretcher!"

"No, Michael. I was the one running behind you, trying to tell you what happened."

"But—"

"I know you must have thought I was the one on the gurney since you saw my jacket over her body."

"Yes, that I did."

"We placed it there, making sure that she stayed warm."

"I see. So what happened?"

"Listen. Nicole and Entyce had just came back to the house. When they were walking up stairs, Nicole was saying how she thought you were over in Puerto Rico, enjoying your Puerto Rican Princess. That's when I came out of our bedroom, ready to knock fire from her ass. Well, she went for her pistol and pulled it out of her purse. As she was trying to aim it at me, I quickly grabbed her by the arm and turned her hand back towards her, causing her to fire one piercing round into her chest."

"Damn."

"Yes. So, we called the ambulance to the house. The heifer was breathing when they got there, but when I pulled up in the Benz, that's when I saw you and the others standing over her body. Is she alright?"

"I don't know. The entire time I thought it was you inside the operating room. Then I heard the nurse say that her mother was here. That's when I knew something wasn't right, due to you telling me that you still haven't found her yet."

"You're right, I haven't. But listen. You're going to have to be strong for the rest of the team. Not only for you and I, but for the group as well. Now please pull yourself together, so that we can join the rest of the team."

"Okay, give me a quick minute," I said to her as I quickly threw some water on my face, making me look as if I hadn't been crying.

"So, whose mother is here; Sharon's or Nicole's?"

"I really don't know. All I know is that everyone else is seated in the waiting room waiting on us. Now bring your ass."

"Yesum," I replied with a smile a million miles long as I reached for her hand.

"Oh no, Mister. Your black ass is still in the dog house with me! You had no damn business putting your dick in that lil' tramp! To tell you the truth, I don't care if she lives or dies!"

"Damn! You for real?"

"Damn skippy, Michael. How would your black ass feel if I had fucked somebody else and then told you that I was having their child instead of yours?"

I placed my head down as we bent a right, walking towards the waiting area.

"Oh no, don't get quiet now. Seriously, how would you feel?"

"Not good."

"I know. See, how that shit feels! Now fix your face and act like you know. We can't let the others see us at each other's neck. But like I said, this shit is not over yet, Mister!"

# CHAPTER 54
## SISTERS!

A few minutes later, Rhynyia and I were seated in the waiting room with everyone else, eagerly awaiting word on Sharon and Nicole. The room was filled with an atmosphere as if we were all at someone's funeral with Reese sitting next to a still crying Entyce. Mignon stood by the entrance, talking it up with Yani. Meanwhile, Strawberry was sitting next to my sister, explaining the gory details of the horrific nightmare that had happened back at the house.

I had just made myself comfortable in my chair when Rhynyia looked over to me and said, "Excuse me real quick while I go to the restroom."

"Yeah, sure, bae. I'll be right here when you get back."

"I know you will," she replied as she stood to walk away. "Redd, you good?"

"Yes, Yani, just going to the ladies's room. I'll be right back. Excuse me," she said as she walked between her and Mignon. She then exited the room, headed to the restroom.

We all looked over at one another, not knowing what to expect next.

Then out of nowhere, one of the doctors came out of the room and uttered, "Okay, it seems as though we were able to revive her. She's breathing comfortably on her own now, but she's not out of the woods just yet."

"Can we see her, doc?" Mignon asked the doctor who stood around five foot nine, weighing a hundred and sixty pounds with black hair and a small mustache over two thin slits that I believe he called lips.

"Not right now. She won't be able to respond to anything at this moment."

"Why? What's her condition?"

Everyone paused for a brief minute with a stunned look as the doctor turned to see the face of who the voices belonged to.

"Excuse me, ma'am, and you are?" the alarmed looking doctor asked.

"I'm her mother."

"What?" Mignon asked me with a whisper.

"Damn, she looks just like Rhynyia,"Strawberry mumbled to herself.

"Oh, I'm so sorry, ma'am. So you are the mother of Ms. Jackson, correct?"

"No, I'm the mother of Ms. Sharon Conoly. Can I please see my daughter?"

"Yes, ma'am. I'm not her doctor. I'm the doctor of Ms. Nicole Jackson. Please follow me while I find you the doctor in charge of your daughter's care."

"Thank you. Hello, Michael. You all must be the ones who helped him rescue my daughter and grandbaby?" Karen said as she tried to smile.

"Hello, ma'am, and yes they are." I then stood up to greet her as everyone else introduced themselves to Sharon's mother.

"Hey, grandma!"

"Hello, Breanna. Let's go see your mother. It was nice meeting you all. Michael, I'll speak with you after I see Sharon. Have you seen her yet?"

"No, ma'am. It seems as though one of the young ladies who works with me had an accident, so we're still waiting to find out her status."

"I see. Well, I'll speak with you when you finish up here. Once again, thank you all for everything you have done," she said as she backed out of the room with Breanna in hand, headed to find the correct doctor.

She had just bent the corner as Strawberry stood up in the middle of the floor with her arm in a sling and said, "Damn, if she doesn't look like her and Rhynyia. They could be sisters."

# CHAPTER 55
## FIRED!

I was just as shocked as everyone else was as I stared at Strawberry and said, "Okay, Berry, sit that flat ass of yours down before Rhynyia comes out and sees you acting out and shit."

"Okay, and what am I not supposed to be seeing, Mister?" Rhynyia asked, as she returned from the restroom.

My head snapped around as I quickly uttered, "Nothing. Just telling her to have a seat before she falls and breaks her other arm."

"Whatever."

"For real," I said to Rhynyia as she took her seat next to me.

"Where is Sharon's daughter?"

"Your... I mean her grandmother just took her to see Sharon."

"Thanks, Strawberry. What were you about to say about 'your'?"

"Nothing. I meant nothing, Sexy Redd," Strawberry replied, trying to cover up her mistake before she had the whole room in a mess.

"Why does everyone have that look on their faces as if they seen a ghost or something?"

"I have no idea." I just sat there not knowing what to do next.

Reese broke the tension and suspense in the waiting room when he stood up and said, "If y'all don't mind, I'm taking Entyce outside for some fresh air."

"No problem, Reese. If anything changes, I'll holla at cha."

"Cool, Mike." We dapped before he placed his arm around Entyce, smiling back at me as they rushed out of the tension filled room.

Strawberry was still focused on how much Rhynyia and Sharon's mom looked a like as her and my sister stood to walk towards the cafeteria.

"Hey, where are you two going?"

"Trying to grab us something to eat, Rhynyia. Hey, listen. Why don't you and Mike head back to the house? If anything changes I'll give you guys a call," my sister voiced.

"Sounds good to me. What about you, Michael?" she said as she looked down at me.

I was still seated in my chair trying to keep calm. "I'm cool with that, just as long as you guys let me know if anything changes with either one of them."

"Yes, Mike. Man, go ahead and get to the house. We will be there as soon as we hear something from both doctors."

I had just stood up, searching for my brother. "Cool. Firstborn, first thing in the morning, get Cynthia to follow you over to Robinson's paint and body shop so that you can drop the truck off to be fixed."

"Gotcha, will do."

"Later, guys."

We had just stepped outside when Rhynyia looked over at me and said, "Just take a load off of them tired ass feet of yours, I'll drive us home."

"Thank you. I do need the rest."

"Get in, boy," Rhynyia voiced as she pushed the alarm button on the car.

"So, we're leaving for Puerto Rico first thing in the morning, right?"

"Nah, today is Tuesday, and you know what that means."

"Hollywood Nites and Apollo South. Besides, the girls think I'm in Puerto Rico. I can't wait until they see us together."

"Oh, you're right. I haven't had a chance to dance at Hollywood Nites yet."

"So, what we'll do is work both clubs tonight, and then leave first thing Wednesday."

"Wait a minute, Mike, what about the Caribbean Beach night club?" she asked me as she made a right onto the interstate.

"Girl, we lost that spot because of Lil' Kittys hot ass," I replied as I laid my head back against my headrest.

"What?"

"Yep, Lil' Kitty did some foul ass shit and they fired us."

# CHAPTER 56
### KILL OR BE KILLED!

It was Tuesday afternoon, a hot and blissful day already, as I finally woke up and ventured downstairs to find myself something to eat. While downstairs I happened to peak out of the kitchen window to see just how nice the sunny day looked, when I spotted the daily newspaper sprawled out across the front lawn. Just as I had turned the paper over, my day in which I had just started only minutes earlier seemed like it was about to be all another bad dream in the life of the man who owned the world-famous Florida Hot Girls.

*Mass shootout at a local Daytona Beach Red Lobster* was written on the cover of the paper. While walking into the house reading what was said, I saw a few pictures of the said assailants but the pictures weren't that good of the individuals in question. As I sat down reading over the article, Rhynyia walked in, only with her see through gown covering up her dazzling naked body with her caramel skin glowing as the bright Florida sun broke through the window curtains, shinning off her. I intuitively took down the paper and asked myself if I should make love to her right here in the living room or take her back upstairs and make love to her in our bed.

It all became an afterthought as she placed her hand on my shoulder and lowered her head and softly kissed my ear. "If the bitch lives, Michael, you know that she can't ever come back here to stay in my damn house. Nor can she be a part of this group any longer. She has to be removed, just like the other bitch, Miss Kitty."

I turned my back to her. "But, Rhynyia, she's part of the Murder Queens. What if she goes to the police and tells them everything that there is to tell about the group?"

"I know, and I've thought about that, too. But the bitch has crossed the line when she fucked my man. There is no way that we can live in the same damn house and I know that she wants to be with you, just as much as I want to be with your black ass!"

"So where does that leave us?" I asked as I stood, looking directly in her cold, calculated eyes.

"I guess that leaves you with the question that you've been asking yourself all morning."

"And what is that?"

"Which one do you choose— me or her, Michael?" Damn, how did she know that my conscience and I were even having that conversation? "I hope you know, Michael, you talk in your sleep." She walked into the kitchen with me tailing right behind her. "I don't know who in the hell you were talking to this morning, but you and whomever were having a very long conversation about choosing between her and me." She then closed the door of the fridge with my conscience standing behind it with an alarming, wicked smile across his face.

"Damn, I didn't know that she was up listening to what you and I were talking about."

"Thanks," I said to my conscience.

Rhynyia turned from the kitchen window and said, "So, you know that this means that we're gonna have to silence her."

"What do you have in mind?"

"You know what I have in mind. I don't even know why you asked me that dumb ass question."

With those words rolling off of her lips, my heart dropped. I never would have imagined one of us taking out one of our very own. The entire time Rhynyia and I were in the kitchen talking about the demise of Nicole, there was someone else upstairs listening to our conversation as I begged and pleaded with Rhynyia to let Nicole have a pass.

"Rhynyia, killing does not come that easy for me as it does for you," I said to her as she began to walk back up to our room.

She had only taken a few steps when the adorable vixen of death turned and said, "Well, where I come from, it's how one becomes the one who sits on top of the food chain! In other words, Mister: Kill or be killed. Make your choice, Michael!"

# CHAPTER 57
## BABY PHAT SHORTS!

After several minutes of going back and forth with Rhynyia about the precious life of Nicole, it was evident that there was no other way around saving her. I could tell by the fire in her eyes and the harsh tone in her voice that Nicole's time here on earth was about to be up. And to think, the sad thing about it all was that Nicole didn't even know what was about to happen to her. Somehow or someone was going to have to get to her before her life as we all knew it was over. I hadn't received word yet on if she woke up from her coma. All I knew was that she was still breathing on her own. We hadn't really said two words to one another since the day I took Sharon out to dinner. If I knew things would have transpired like they did, I would have spoken to her every day in order to save her cherished life.

While walking out of the shower, I was thinking that I had to get away for a few hours so that I could clear my head. I eased over to the bed where Rhynyia lay, watching television, and gently kissed her on her cheek.

She looked up at me with that same fire still in her eyes. "So, where do you think you're going, Mister?"

"I have a few errands to tend to before we leave for Tampa tonight. Besides, if I'm supposed to be leaving tomorrow for Puerto Rico, I definitely have to make sure things are in order before I leave," I replied as I walked towards the closet to find something to wear.

"I see. Well, should I get dressed so that I can come with you."

"No, I'm only going to be away for a few hours or so." I dabbed my face with some of my Jope cologne while she sat up in bed, gazing at me, studying my every move. I dully turned towards her and said, "Is there something I can help you with, young lady?"

"No, I just hope you take what I said downstairs serious, Michael."

"Rhynyia, I heard you, but do you seriously think killing her is going to change everything?"

She immediately jumped off the bed, staring me directly in my face. "I guess you don't seem to fucking understand, Michael. That bitch you care so much about tried to kill me. Do you think that she was just trying to shoot me to scare me? That lil' tramp pulled out her weapon and was trying to kill me over you. Now, if you don't understand that, fuck you and her!" She then slammed our bedroom door in my face as she stormed out.

As she ran downstairs, headed to I don't know where, I tried to run behind her when Yani grabbed me by my arm and said, "Michael, let her go right now. I'll speak with her. Now go take care of yo business."

"Thanks, Yani." I then pulled her into me, hugging her tightly.

Minutes later, I was walking back out of my bedroom dressed to impress. I was walking downstairs when I passed by Mignon who was going up with a fruit salad in her hand. She looked up to see me as she said, "Good afternoon, Michael. Don't you look nice. Where are you headed?"

"Thank you, Mignon. Just out to handle some Florida Hot Girl Business before I have to leave for Puerto Rico. How are you doing?"

"Fine. Just a lil' sore. I guess I'll be alright after I get some rest."

"Well if you don't won't to go tonight, you know that you can always take tonight off."

"Not tonight. You know damn well tonight is Tuesday at Hollywood, and that's when everybody comes out to get their groove on!" She placed a gentle smile on her face.

"Okay, well I'll be back in a few hours. See you then."

"Alright, Michael, you be safe," she said to me as she turned to walk back upstairs with half her nice ass hanging out of her Baby Phat cut-off shorts.

# CHAPTER 58
## TAKE HER LIFE!

While walking throughout the living room, headed to the garage, I decided to check on my sister who was supposed to be sleeping in one of the guest bedrooms. I softly walked up on the door of the room and gently knocked twice. A few seconds went by with no answer, so I tapped louder, harder the second time. Still no answer. So, I mildly pushed open the door to find her already up and gone. But where? She told me earlier that she would be in Orlando all day, waiting to see what the news would report about the shooting earlier that morning deep off inside that muddy ass swamp.

I shrugged her absence off as I went to the garage to choose from the assortment of vehicles to ride in that day. I noticed the Denali gone, so I figured that my sister had followed my brother over to Robinson's Paint and Body to drop the truck off. There was only a choice of vehicle that I wanted to drive that very hot afternoon, which was my black big body Mercedes. As I turned the ignition and heard the way it purred, I felt a calm come over my body, causing me to have a bit more placidity and serenity about myself. I meekly eased out of the garage hoping that Rhynyia and I could have been on better terms before leaving the house. But by the way she had exploded on me, I knew that a little time away from one another would probably be better for the both of us.

As I made a left turn, headed out of the elegant gated community we resided in, I eased over my console, searching through my CD collection for something to listen to when I happened to fumble upon a CD that had *play me* written on it. I then slid it inside the Boise Stereo system to hear the song *25 Reasons* by Nivea. I looked back at the cover to see that it had Rhynyia's handwriting on the cover. I guess she wanted me to really know how she felt about me.

As I listened to the lyrics of the song, it dawned on me that in just the short time I had known Rhynyia, I had never seen her that angry side of her until that afternoon. I guess since her life had been put in jeopardy, she felt some type of way, and I couldn't blame her. Hell, if someone would have pulled a gun out on me, I would have felt the same way.

I merged onto John Young Parkway, headed to the hospital. I had to see Sharon first so that I could make sure she was alright. Then I would be off to see Nicole to see if there had been any changes to her condition. It really didn't matter what her condition was, I knew what I had to do now. I was given a direct order by the head female of the Florida Hot Girls. The only problem I had was the mere fact of me being able to be the one to take her life. Damn, now here it was, all put on my head. And to think, I was the one who brought her into the group. Now I would be the one to take her out. It had to be another way. Only if I could have figured one out before I reached the hospital.

# CHAPTER 59
## STILL BREATHING!

Chief Trevor B. Jones of the Bridgeville Police Department was just getting to the crime scene. He had been with the department for only a few years. After years of corruption in the department, Chief Jones was transferred from the Medulla Police Department to fix the problems internally.

The forensic lab was taping off the horrific scene. Chief Jones stood around six foot three and weighed somewhere around two hundred and ten pounds. Light skinned with a clean-shaven bald head. He maintained his fat-free, physically fit body through his military-style workouts that he did faithfully once a day before the break of dawn.

"Chief, it looks like they put up a good fight before they got sidetracked by whatever weapons the bad guys had," one of the officers on the scene voiced.

The Chief bent down, sliding the white sheet off one of his slain police officers. "How long ago do you think this gunfight took place?"

"By the looks of things here, Chief, about seven hours ago."

"Who else knows about what happened here? And are there any witnesses?" the Chief asked as he stood back up.

"You're not going to believe this Chief, but there are a few rednecks, I mean guys, over there, dressed in Klansman gear. They say that they were a part of the melee."

"What?" Chief Jones replied by turning to look over in the direction of the five men who looked like they had been through hell and back. When he saw the line of guys up against their old beat-up Ford pickup trucks, he automatically knew what to expect next.

As he mutely walked over to talk with the red necks aligning their vehicles, one of his fellow officers shouted from across the swampy area, "Hey, Chief, we got something over here!"

Before the Chief could even get halfway to where the officer was standing, another officer yelled, "Chief, looks like we have a serious problem!"

"And what is that?" the Chief asked as he stopped dead in his tracks, placing his hands on his waist in disgust.

"Look like all these guys were officers from your department," the short, white ,stubby officer with the fat reddish face said to Chief Jones while chewing on a freshly baked Bear Claw doughnut.

"Do you have the officers' names?"

"Yes, sir. It looks like what's left of officer Stephan Murray. Then there's officer Kyle Williams and Roman Waonoski dead over there near the end of the swamp. What the bullets didn't do to them, the alligators did the rest," the officer said as he continued eating the doughnut, standing there looking over the half-eaten bodies of his fellow slain officers.

"Well, I be John Brown. What in the hell were these crooked ass cops of mine doing out here in the middle of this dense looking swamp, and without back up?" Chief Jones asked as he turned away from the badly decomposed bodies, headed back to the men aligning their trucks.

Meanwhile, to the left of the abysmal crime scene, one of the female forensic lab technicians made a gruesome discovery. "Oh my God, we have two live ones over here!" she shouted.

The officers in attendance ran towards where she was standing.

"Chief! Hey, Chief, looks like they're still breathing!"

# CHAPTER 60
## HAVING YOUR CHILD!

As I eased into the hospital parking lot, I was still feeling a bit apprehensive about doing what Rhynyia wanted me to do. I knew that she meant business, but I also knew that I was not the man for the job. Needless to say, Nicole meant the world to me, and I just couldn't put myself to the task of killing her. It wasn't like when I had taken out Do-Dirty; it was all different. Do-Dirty tried to steal from me, whereas Nicole tried to kill the woman of my dreams. I sat still as if I was a living corpse in my car for a brief minute, debating on what should I do, when I saw Sharon's mother and Breanna walking out of the hospital headed towards her car. I paused because I didn't want them to see me. Once I made sure that they were a few miles away, I walked into the gift shop and purchased a nice arrangement of flowers for Sharon and Nicole. I then grayly walked up to the register.

The cashier said, "Will there be anything else, sir?"

"Yes, where is the baby oil?"

"Right here, sir. We carry that behind the counter. Do you want a small bottle or large?"

"Make it a large bottle, please."

"Yes, sir." She then rang up the total as she smiled. "Thirty-five, sixty-seven, sir."

"Here you go." I handed her two twenties and then waited for my change.

"Here you go, sir, and have a nice day."

"Thank you." I walked towards the door with my items in hand.

Since I knew that Nicole hadn't woken up from her coma as of yet, I decided to go to her room first. If I was going to kill her, I might as well get it over with. I mumbled to myself as I nervously walked in the direction of her room.

I had just walked up on her room door and softly eased in, not wanting to make a sound. The room was somewhat dark and a bit cool as I numbly walked in with the intentions of placing the baby oil in her IV tube. She looked so harmless and calm as she lay in her bed, not knowing what I had come to do to her. As I stood over her, gazing at how beautiful and innocent she looked, tears began to snake down my face.

"Damn, I can't do this to you," I whispered to myself.

Then suddenly, as if I was in a movie and was the lead character, the song *I Will Always Love You* by the late, great Whitney Houston came on behind me. I quickly turned around to see my sister seated in a chair in the back of the room, hidden in the darkness with a loaded three eighty pointed at me. I abruptly dropped the flowers and said, "What are you doing here, and with a gun pointed at me?"

"I should be asking you the same thing, Baby Boy! But we know why," she said as she emerged from the dark.

"Yeah, I didn't expect to see you here."

"I know. I wouldn't be here, but I overheard you and the Princess talking about killing her. So, I had to come down here and at least try to somehow warn her of what was to come."

"Yeah, I hear you, but what if Nicole had gotten off her shot? Poor Rhynyia didn't have anyone to warn her."

"Listen, Baby Boy, I fully understand where you and her are coming from. But no one has to die. Just let the doctors take care of her, and then I'll have her to relocate somewhere like she planned before all this happened."

"Yeah, I wish it was that simple, big sis. But Rhynyia wants her dead, and you know how tenacious she can be if she doesn't get her way," I replied as I slid out the bottle of baby oil.

"Mike, please. Let's think this over understandingly. What you are about to do to this poor girl is irrational. This girl is carrying your baby, and she loves you with all of her heart. You can't kill her and walk away from it like nothing ever happened!"

# CHAPTER 61
### PAIN MEDICATIONS!

I stood firm as I stared into the dark eyes of my sister. "Listen, I never meant for any of this to get this far, but let's be sensible here. If she lives through this ordeal, she's gonna want revenge, and I can't let her come back and succeed at killing Rhynyia!"

"Mike, once she gets better, I'll move her to another country. She will be so far away that no one will ever know what happened to her."

By now I was slowly moving over to the IV slowly dripping into her veins.

My sister had moved between the IV and the bed, pleading for me to think about what I was about to do, when she nonchalantly slid back the chamber on her weapon and said, "Step back, Michael. I'm warning you."

"So, damn, let me get this straight. You're going to shoot me just like that?" I gave her a wicked smile.

She pulled on the same smile. "I'm prepared to do whatever I have to do to keep my group of fierce ladies together."

"You see, that's the problem. They were supposed to be my girls until you filled their heads up with that bullshit about being some elite group of ladies called the Murder Queens, who go around killing people for hire! Like some assassins and shit."

"It wasn't bullshit that night that they saved your ass over in Saint Petersburgh, was it?" she growled while still pointing her three eighty at me.

"No, it wasn't, but I just can't have them going around killing people. Hell, that shit is going to get me sent to prison for a very long time. And you and I both know that I'm not built for prison life!" I shouted back at her, furious now that I was even put in a situation like I was.

"Okay, I see where you're coming from. The girls will tone it down."

"But we still have the small problem of Nicole."

"Mike, let me put my gun down. Promise me that you won't harm her. And then let's go somewhere and talk about what you are about to do here."

"Shit, you pulled your gun out on me, and to think we're supposed to be family."

"C'mon, Mike, do you actually think that I would pull a loaded gun out on my own flesh and blood? This damn thing isn't even loaded. Plus, I would shoot myself before I would shoot my own brother," she said to me while placing her gun down on Nicole's bed.

We embraced one another with a hug and then I moved back, still keeping my eyes on my sister. "Give me about an hour, and we'll go from there."

"Cool. Thanks, Baby Boy. I know you couldn't kill her!" she said to me as I calmly walked towards the door of the room.

But just as I reached the doorknob, I heard her call out my name. "Michael." I briskly turned around to see her trying to open her eyes and hear her first words utter from her precious small ass mouth. "Michael, where am I?" Nicole asked me while trying to move her aching limbs.

I immediately rushed back to her bedside, placing the bottle of baby oil in my pants pocket and then reaching for her outstretched hand. My sentimental ass sister gently moved out of my path while wiping away her tears that had begun to flow down her face. "You're in the hospital, Nicole."

"The hospital?" she said, sounding all groggy from all of the pain medication they had her on.

# CHAPTER 62
## BREAKING ANOTHER HEART!

She then tried moving around in her bed as she fixed her eyes on the sight of me standing there.

"Yes, you tried to shoot Rhynyia and shot yourself in the chest by mistake."

Tears began to form in the well of her eyes as the nurses and doctors ran into her room, checking on her vital signs. "My baby. How is my baby?" she began to shout, as the nurses and doctors tried to calm her down, fearing that she would tear out the IV stuck in her arm.

I quietly backed out of the room to let them do what they had to do. Just as I closed the door behind me, I placed my head down and walked back down the hallway, headed towards Sharon's room, but the closer I got, the louder the commotion was becoming from the emergency entrance.

I reached her door seconds later and then stopped in my tracks when I saw damn near the whole entire police force and half of the paramedics bringing in two badly burned police officers. The one gurney had one officer on it screaming and yelling about how much pain he was in, while the second gurney had another officer on it. But his face was so badly burned that I almost threw up in my mouth just by looking at him.

As the orderlies pushed the gurney by me, I heard one of his fellow officers say out loud, "They say it looked like the bad guys had a Grenade Launcher, and that's what blew off half the face of Lieutenant Richards!"

I snapped my head around in sheer disbelief and whispered, "Fuck, that son of a bitch didn't die after all." When I turned around, I could see him frantically moving his hand around, trying to feel for the part of his face that was partially missing.

Chief Trevor Jones walked in behind the barrage of police officers, pissed to the highest of pissed off levels one could be when he shouted out, "Get me all the details of what transpired out there between my officers and the army they had the shootout with! I want all available officers working around the clock in order to find out what in the hell happened!"

After I saw the anger in his face, I knew then that it was far from being over for me and the Murder Queens. Now we would have to fight the whole entire police department because some of their own had been violently taken out.

I had to get out of the hospital, quick, fast and in a hurry, so I quickly pulled one of the nurses over to the side and said, "Excuse me, could you please give these flowers to the young lady in the room right behind us?"

She looked down at the flowers and then back up at me, smiling with her fast grown ass. "Certainly. Should I say who they're from?"

I smiled in return. "Yes, tell her they're from the man of her dreams!" I then handed her a crisp hundred-dollar bill and dashed for the door.

"Damn, you don't want my number so you can be the man of my dreams too!"

I laughed to myself as I ran out to the parking lot. There were things I still had to tend to before I left for Puerto Rico. And breaking the heart of another beautiful woman wasn't one of them!

# CHAPTER 63
## KILL HER!

At the Vallentino estate, Rhynyia and Yani sat at the pool, looking up into the nice clear blue sky. It was a nice, hot, sunny day in beautiful Orlando, Florida. The temperature was somewhere around eighty-four degrees, but it felt like a hundred as the gorgeous duo lounged around the pool in their beautiful bathing suits. Yani was wearing a nice two-piece pink ensemble with all of her beautiful Haitian body protruding out of what she had on. Rhynyia had on a black and red bathing suit with it barely being able to cover up her fat ass along with her nice full size breast that were hanging out of her bra.

Mignon saw both at the pool from the kitchen window and yelled, "Hey, is the water cold enough?"

"Yes, girl, why don't you bring your scary ass out here and find out for yourself!" Rhynyia yelled back to her.

Yani looked over at Rhynyia and then asked her, "So, you're alright now, Princess?"

"Yes, I guess I'll be alright… When he gets back and has done what I asked him to do!" She slowly sipped on her tall cold glass of Iced Tea.

"You know dat he really love you, Rhynyia," Yani voiced, as she slid down her Chanel shades, staring Rhynyia directly in her eyes.

"Well, if he loves me so fucking much, he wouldn't be going around sticking his dick in everything that moves around here!" Rhynyia said with a bit of anger and jealously in her voice.

"You right, but you jus can't blame everyting on Michael. You know it takes two to fuck up."

"I feel you, Yani, but how would his ass feel if I fucked everything that walked around me?"

"Dat's de difference between a man and a woman, Princess. If we do as dey do, den we become a hoe. But dey can fuck who dey want and jus be dawgs, and fo some strange reason, we still love dem de same."

"Well not me, Yani. this is Michael's last damn time. If I find out that he has more sex partners than just me, I'm done. My child and I will be out of his life so fucking fast that his whole life would be changed in a matter of minutes."

"Damn, you serious bout dat shit, huh?"

"Serious as a heart attack."

Minutes later, Mignon walked outside in a nice brand-new two-piece Baby Phat bathing suit with her long pretty, black silky hair pulled up in a bun so that it wouldn't get wet as she pranced across the outer area of the pool for Yani and Rhynyia to see how beautiful she looked.

"Girl, stop it I say," Rhynyia shouted as she stood up to place her arms around Mignon's neck.

"Shut yo' mouth, bitches. I know y'all see all of this fine ass walking around in front of y'all."

They laughed as they all stood around the pool, admiring how nice they all looked in their bathing suits.

"Mignon, where did you get that Baby Phat bathing suit from?" Rhynyia asked, pouring herself some more tea.

"Girl, this lil' thing? I think I picked it up a few weeks ago. You know we travel some of everywhere, and I seem to have forgotten where I got it from!" she replied as they continued to chop it up amongst themselves. Mignon then broke the tension in the air when she said, "Hey, Rhynyia. I kind of overheard you and Michael talking earlier about disposing of one of the girls in the group."

"Yes, you did, Mignon. And I meant that shit, too. If anyone feels different than I do, they can haul ass with her!"

"Listen, I feel you, but Nicole saved Michael's life a few months ago while we were involved in some type of situation with two dumb ass niggas down in St. Pete."

"What?" Rhynyia's mouth was wide open with surprise at what she was hearing.

"Yes. We had just left Apollo South and were dancing at some lil' pool hall-slash-club. When we got there, things were fine until one of the guys got mad because the girls were not allowed to fuck anything."

"Okay, keep going. What happened next?"

"Well, while we were all inside dancing, Michael went out back to talk with the guys about the ladies not fucking for any money. That's when one of the guys pulled out an AK-47 and pointed the damn thing at his head, demanding all of their money back. We didn't know what was going on until Nicole told us to follow her outside. Needless to say, she took matters in her own hand and took care of the problem. We all walked out of there that night with our lives. So, you see Rhynyia, we have to give her a pass and work this problem out between one another so we can keep this group together as a fucking family."

Rhynyia then put her head down and began to walk away.

# CHAPTER 64
### HER MOUTH!

4:45 PM I had just pulled up at Robinson's Paint and Body shop to check on my vehicle. I passively stepped out of the Benz and shouted to one of the guys sand-blasting a very beat up black Denali. "Excuse me! Is Lil' Jeff inside?"

"Yeah, he's inside his office."

"Thanks, my man."

"Don't mention it, Mr. Vallentino," he uttered as I walked inside to find Lil' Jeff, busy on the phone talking with one of his customers.

Lil Jeff cut a smile at me as I eased through his office door. He then threw up his index finger and whispered, "Give me a quick minute."

"Sure, Jeff, do you," I replied as I sat down.

Jeff was about five nine and weighed around a hundred and seventy-five pounds soaking wet. He had light green eyes to go along with his light brown complexion. He always wore his hair in a short fade-like haircut. Some would say that he was a ladies' man, but since the brother was married, he always kept it professional around the ladies. Until one night at one of our off-the-wall bachelor parties.

As I sat there listening to him on the phone, I thought back to the time when it seemed as though one of his college frat brothers were getting married and he wanted the world-famous Florida Hot Girls for their entertainment to make his last night a most memorable one. And that's exactly what they did. The show was held at one of the nicest resorts in Orlando. Lake Buena Vista Resorts right off of Turkey Lake Road. I had at least thirteen girls with me that wild and crazy night. The lineup consisted of everyone's favorite girl, Ms. Bad Ass Tarshay, of course Mignon, Sexy Redd, Lil' Red, Strawberry, Suga Bear, Chazz, lil' hot booty ass Lil' Kitty, Charlie B, Nicole, Entyce, Peekachu, and JK. Not to mention this one new chick that I had met earlier in the week by the name of Monique who decided to show up a lil' later. She just had to make her grand entrance into the group by being a lil' tardy to the party.

Now the night was good until the girls got a lil' tipsy and really turned things up a notch. As usual the ladies were not allowed to participate in anything sexual, but you know as well as I do that once my black ass allowed Tarshay and her bag of tricks to come, all rules were immediately thrown out of the door.

As I was walking around making sure that everyone was doing okay, I happened to walk in one of the rooms to see Chazz with someone's manhood submerged deep inside her mouth. I was just as shocked as you when I shouted to her, "Chazz, what in the hell are you doing?"

Without missing a stroke, she turned her full mouth in my direction and replied, "It doesn't look like it seems."

"Oh, I get it. He was just walking by and his dick somehow just fell into your open mouth, right?"

She kept right on slurping, and nonchalantly shook her head. Then she took his manhood by the base and pulled it out. "Something like that."

I was closing the door on her hot ass when I turned back and shouted, "You know that ass has a fat ass fine when you get through with all of that meat inside your mouth!"

"Whatever, Mike, I gotcha!" she replied and kept right on doing her.

I honestly believe that was the very first time I caught her with something in her mouth, besides a damn blunt.

# CHAPTER 65
## BEAUTY ON BEAUTY!

Now as I journeyed throughout the massive hotel, checking on my ladies, I spotted Lil' Kitty over in the corner of one of the rooms with her thin ass thong wrapped around this one guy's fat ass neck. "Lil' Kitty, why in the hell are you butt ass naked?" I shouted.

She turned her small, frail body around, looking at me as if I was crazy for asking her that. "Because he's breaking bread, Mike! Don't you see all this money in between these fine ass legs?"

I happened to look down between her legs, and she was absolutely right. Between those two thin legs that looked like chicken legs was a pile of money. "Oh, my bad. Stay naked then. But please make sure that you add my fine in your tip out fee for your lil' skinny ass being butt naked."

"Whatever, Mike. You know this pussy looks good. It would even look better sitting on those small ass lips that you have on your face."

"Shut the fuck up, Lil' Kitty!" I yelled back to her as I ventured out to the balcony to see Charlie B backing her nice fat red ass on this ugly ass nigga from Tallahassee, Florida.

"What's up, Mike? You good?" she asked as a smile emerged on her face.

"Nothing, just making sure that you were doing alright," I replied while stepping over to the side of the balcony, looking out over the luxurious resort.

"She's good, dawg. I got her fine ass all night. And I'm throwing nothing but twenties on her fine ass all night long," the not-so nice on the eyes big brute yelped.

I bluntly turned to look down between her legs to see the floor covered with nothing but twenty-dollar bills. "Do your thing, Charlie B!"

"Gotcha, Mike," she said as I walked away smiling at her and her large amount of money.

So, while still canvassing the whole entire suite that night, I walked off into another portion of the huge room to find my Sexy Redd dancing on top of a table with about five guys surrounding it, throwing all kind of money at her fine, caramel looking ass. I stood there startled and mystified for a minute or two with my back up against the wall, watching how she was mesmerizing her small crowd of thirsty ass men when Lil' Jeff walked up to me from around the corner.

"Hey, Mike, I think that I want her inside the VIP room with me."

I looked back at him with a surprised look on my face. "Her? The one on the table right there?"

"Yes, my man. The one that y'all call Sexy Redd."

I then smiled at him as I took the red cherry flavored blow pop out of my mouth. "So sorry to burst your bubble Lil' Jeff. That one there is all mine!" I was still smiling at him when he looked at me and put his head down and walked away.

Minutes later I saw him walk into the bathroom with Monique right behind his lil' short ass. Now I don't know what those two did that night, but whatever it was, she came out with enough money to pay her rent for up to six months. After standing there for about ten minutes watching Sexy Redd, I walked off into another part of the room to witness Nicole and Mignon dancing in the middle of the floor butt naked. Now what a pretty sight to see, because five minutes later into their routine, short, thick ass Tarshay decided that she wanted to start the pussy-eating festivities off before I could even make the announcement.

She gently laid Mignon down and began eating her beautiful shaven pussy, while Nicole down above Mignon's face. Man, when I tell you how them three ladies had all of them guys going crazy in that room that night, it was a sight to see. Beauty on beauty, eating on some nice ass pussy.

# CHAPTER 66
## TAKING CARE OF NICOLE!

Now I would be dead wrong not to tell you all where your girl Strawberry was that night, but it was totally off limits. Needless to say, she was where she wished she would have never been.

It seems as though ole berry got herself a lil' tipsy and staggered into the wrong damn room. I peeked in that room and saw what those two Mandingo-looking niggas were doing to your girl. I had to run out so that I could catch my breath after I saw what she was going through. I must admit though, ole Berry walked away with a pretty penny that night, after she took all of that pressure those two had put on her ass. After being in the room for about two hours with them two brothers, ole Berry took the rest of the night off. She would go on to tell me later that it had to do something with them brothers blowing her back out.

*That was one wild and crazy night*, I thought as I waited for Lil' Jeff to finish his conversation.

I was still smiling to myself when he hung up the phone and slid me the cost for me to have my truck fixed. He cut a half smile at me and then asked me the million-dollar question. "Yo, Mike, when are we going to do another show?"

"Whenever you feel like spending that bread!"

We then walked outside to my car. We stood outside for a minute or so as he marveled at what I had pulled up in.

As I stepped inside my car, he casually slid his head inside to check out the interior of the fine foreign automobile. "Boy, when I grow up, I want to be just like you," he uttered while smiling at the beautiful black Mercedes Benz that I had sitting at his place of business.

"Shut up, Jeff. As much money as you're making here, you can buy at least five of these things and still have some money to throw around."

"Whatever, playa. When you pulled up, I thought you were one of the Magic Players."

"Yeah, Jeff. I'll have Mignon come by later on in the week to pick my truck up." I closed my door and pulled off, headed for the house. I noticed that my phone had like five missed calls. I picked the phone up not wanting to see that it was no one but Rhynyia calling, and I knew what she wanted to know. Had I taken care of Nicole yet.

# CHAPTER 67
## BABY MAMMA!

I pulled out of the parking lot and made a left turn onto Old Winter Garden Road, headed straight for Metro West, trying to come up with some type of lie to tell Rhynyia about me not killing Nicole. "Fuck it! I'll just have to hear her mouth when I get there," I mumbled to myself as I ran the red light at Kirkman Road, trying to get home before she realized that I hadn't taken out Nicole and went to the hospital herself to do the deadly deed.

As I pulled up into my driveway, I noticed that my sister had made it back home, so I didn't know what to expect as I timidly walked into the house. Just as I walked in and took a look around, I knew that something was off. Things just didn't feel right. So, I took off for my room, not alerting anyone that I was home.

As soon as I opened my bedroom door, she ran from the bathroom, screaming, "Michael, why haven't you picked up your phone? I've been worried sick about your black ass all day! I thought that maybe the police had picked you up for killing Nicole!" She had a bit of panic in her eyes and sincerity in her meek voice.

I held my head down as she continued to chastise me as if I was her child or something. Then I looked up into her eyes with mine beginning to water. "Rhynyia, about Nicole."

"Michael, say no more. That's why I was trying to call you."

"What? You wanted to know had I killed her yet, right?"

"Something like that." She said as she turned and walked towards the window of our room, folding her arms over her slight belly bump.

"Something like what, Rhynyia? What happened?"

"Michael, I'm sorry."

"No, Rhynyia, please tell me what you're talking about."

"That I didn't want you to kill your other baby mamma?"

I couldn't say a word as she swiftly turned back to me with that look of anger in her face. "No, Rhynyia."

"No, what, Michael? Whatever. Don't say a word. The reason I was trying to call your black ass is because I changed my mind about killing her. That's why. Now did you kill her?"

"No! I just couldn't bring myself to do it. And on top of that, my sister was there already, waiting on me. She overheard us talking about it earlier this morning."

"What?"

"Yes, she was there, trying to save her life. Protecting her as if Nicole was her child."

"For real?"

"Yes, have you seen her? Her car is out front."

"No, Mignon told me about the night you almost got killed because of the girls, and how Nicole stepped in and saved your life. So, I decided to give her a pass."

"Thanks, Rhynyia. I'm glad you changed your mind."

"Whatever. She still has to apologize to me, Michael."

"Okay, bae. I'll make sure that she does. Do you want to go see her before we leave tomorrow?"

"I don't know. Let me think about that. In the meantime, let's all go get something to eat before we have to leave for the club."

We embraced and then kissed each other as if it was our very first time locking lips.

"Let me have Mignon call and tell Richard to meet us at the house with his crew of girls so that we can all travel down to Tampa together."

"No problem, baby. I'm going to jump in the shower. I've been at the pool half the day with Yani and Mignon. Feel free to join me if you like," she said as she winked at me.

# CHAPTER 68
## HERO!

That mid evening my contact with the channel eleven news team received the scoop of her young lifetime. I knew her personally so I called her and let her in on a hot story so that she could have the jump on the rest of the media sharks. Chief Trevor Jones wanted to keep the incident quiet until they had come up with a scenario to tell the public. In other words, he didn't want the public to know about the crooked cops that he had on his embattled police force. Besides, with half of Lieutenant Richards' face being blown, Sharon would have not been able to identify her kidnapper. Meaning that he and his corrupt cop friends would have gotten away with murder. That's when I called in a favor to my dear friend Ms. Tasha Willis.

Rhynyia and I had just walked out of the shower when my sister yelled upstairs to us. "Hey, now that you two are out of the shower, making love, turn your television on channel eleven!"

"Damn, what is it now?" I shouted back as Rhynyia searched for the remote so that she could turn the television on.

"This is Tasha Willis with breaking news for Channel Eleven News. We're here at the site where Ms. Sharon Conoly and her three-year-old daughter were held for the last two days. Everything came to an abrupt halt earlier this morning here in this swamp of Sanford, Florida. It seems as though they were held by a group of very corrupt police officers of the Bridgeville Police Department. This its remote camp site used by different organizations to hold different kinds of meetings. The local residents here say that it's usually meetings held by the infamous KKK. The area you see behind me, Denise, is located deep in a very swamps of Sanford, that most people would've not even known that it back here unless someone actually brought you here. We had to travel at least five miles off road to get here. And once we did, there was no way for someone to have found it unless with the help of trained guide dogs."

"Do you know the name of the officers that were involved in this crime, Tasha?"

"Not quite yet, Denise. The names of the officers are being withheld until their families are contacted, but we do know that at least two of them are still alive, with three of the five being shot and killed here earlier this morning. On a brighter note, Ms. Conoly and her daughter are doing fine back at Orlando Regional with non-life threatening injuries."

"Now, Tasha, do we know who rescued Ms. Conoly and her young daughter?"

"No, not at the present moment, Denise, and that remains a mystery here among the residents and the police officers that responded to this horrific crime scene this morning. The local residents said that all they saw was a black SUV leaving the crime scene in an awful hurry. We do know this though, Denise. Whomever the people were that rescued Ms. Conoly and her daughter are considered to be heroes for their effort that they put forth in finding Ms. Conoly and her daughter. This has been Tasha Willis reporting for Channel Eleven News."

"So, you're a hero now, huh, Michael?"

"Nah, Rhynyia, I'm just the man who went to save someone special in my heart."

"Okay, don't get your teeth knocked out, Mister! Now let's get dressed so we can get something to eat."

# CHAPTER 69
## LIKE SHARON!

Two hours later, my cousin Richard was pulling up at the house with his crew of girls while Firstborn was out picking up the crew of females that we would be taking to Tampa. Richard's eyes were big ass half silver dollars as he burst through through front door and saw me standing in the kitchen with my plate of food in hand. "Damn cousin. What? You already back from Puerto Rico?" He displayed an invigorating smile as he stood there waiting for my reply.

"Nah, silly ass boy. I had to put it off for tomorrow. Something of importance came up."

"I see. So did you know about your girl Sharon being kidnapped?"

"Yes, Richard. That's why I had to stay back."

"So you were the one who rescued her and her daughter, weren't you?"

"Nah, Rich. I was here at the house when we found out. What would make you think that I was capable of rescuing her?" I asked him as I walked past him, trying to get to the living room with my plate of food.

"Whatever, nigga. You act like I don't know about you and them females that call themselves the Murder Queens."

I quickly turned to him as he stood in the kitchen with his back to me due to him searching for the biggest piece of yard bird to sink his teeth into. "Richard, what did you just say?"

He turned to me with a thick ass piece of chicken in his hand, smiling like he had all the answers. "I said that you think that I don't know about you and them bad ass females that you have, called the Murder Queens."

I gently placed my plate down on the marble counter. "Seriously, my brother, why and what would make you think something like that?

He began chewing on his piece of chicken while spilling crumbs over the floor. "Mike, c'mon man. Tell the truth. Every time something comes up or happens within the circle of this group, them females pop up on the scene."

"Okay, did the police say those were the females who rescued Sharon and her daughter?" I asked him with an authentic look on my face.

"They didn't have to. As soon as I found out that she was missing, people in her family began to call me, telling me this and saying that. Then her aunt told me that her mother told her that…" He stopped mid-sentence as he saw Rhynyia and Yani walking downstairs. With his eyes glued on them, he leaned into me and whispered, "Mike, is that Sharon, or someone who looks like an older version of her?"

I turned slightly to witness Rhynyia waltzing downstairs with Yani by her side. *Oh, shit, he hadn't seen Rhynyia, so I had to think quick on my feet.* "My bad. Excuse me, Richard, this is Rhynyia, my girlfriend. And the lovely lady beside her is my close friend Yani."

He dropped his chicken on the floor as Rhynyia hit him with her gorgeous smile. Then she opened her mouth with, "Well, hello, Richard. Mike has told me so much about you. It's nice to finally meet you."

Yani came back with, "Nice to meet you as well, Richard."

"Same here. I must say, Mike did mention you— Rhynyia, is it?"

"Yes."

"Okay, but he never told me that you were that damn beautiful. And you too, Yani."

They continued smiling at him as they walked past him into the kitchen.

"Thank you, Richard. Mike, is everything here? The baby and I are starving?"

Richard was really tripping now. Rhynyia had just let it be known that she was hungry along with our unborn child.

"Yes, bae, everything is all there. Eat as much as you like."

"That I am. What time is everyone getting here?"

"Richard's crew is already here, outside. And Firstborn should be here within the next few minutes with my crew."

"Okay, that should give me enough time to grab a quick bite."

"Cuz, where has she been the whole damn time that you have been with Sharon?"

"She had to go back home when her brother got killed."

"So, that's Sexy Redd?"

"Yes, now close your damn mouth and pick up that piece of chicken you dropped on my damn floor!"

"Cuz, she is fine as hell. And she's pregnant, too?"

"Yes, Rich. Why?"

"Man, you are a baby-making ass nigga. And oh, by the way, do you know Rhynyia looks exactly like Sharon?"

Everything inside that damn house at that very moment went eerily silent for me right then. I stood frozen stiff with my life flashing before my eyes. Here it was that my first cousin that I loved with all my heart and trusted with my life, had me feeling like I was getting close to the grave. I knew I shouldn't have let him that close to me and my growing empire. How could I have slipped up and trusted him that much? So much that now this lame ass nigga knew my most darkest secrets.

I couldn't even think straight as I played back inside my head what he had said only minutes ago. "*So you were the one who rescued Sharon and her daughter weren't you?"* I had quickly shot back at him that it wasn't me who had rescued her, trying my best to walk past him and into my living room with my plate of food. That's when the lame came back at me with, *"Whatever, nigga. You act like I don't know about you and them females that call themselves the Murder Queens."* At that moment I knew that I had been caught up and now this nigga was gambling with his life.

He was even saying the same thing that I had heard one of the females in the group saying that whenever something popped off with the ladies, the Murder Queens would show up and handle business. After playing that over inside my head it was now the fact that Richard had saw Rhynyia for the first time and even said that she looked like an older version of Sharon. What in the hell was I to do now, with him knowing all of this? If he knew about the Murder Queens it would only be a matter of time before he put two and two together and figured out that it was them and myself who had taken out his thirsty ass baby mamma. Then they would probably figure out that it was me who gave the order for the removal of her and Sharon's uncle— Bernard *Fats* Walker, a brother who the police still hadn't found yet. Dead or alive. They couldn't. Hell, his ass was somewhere stanking right about now right beside his gay ass home boy, who Yani said was named Leroy. Come to think about it, she never did tell me the story of why my brother killed both of them and then smashed their ass up together in some raggedy ass bucket of a car. Oh well, at least both are somewhere resting comfortably together.

With the dire info that Richard knew now I had to ask myself the question: What if his ass went and told Sharon everything he knew? How would her lil' fine red ass react? Now knowing that her intuition was right all along about me and my ladies knowing what happened to her lil' cousin Do-Dirty and Bernard. She would even be closer with her assumption now since she saw the picture of Yani from the two crooked cops the Queens killed. It was the face of the same girl that Sharon's head lay in the night she was rescued. Now here it was that I stood with all kind of mad, diabolical thoughts, racing through my complex mind. A trait I had inherited from my dear parents.

While I slowly tossed my thoughts around I still didn't hear all of the noise and commotion from the girls and Richard. I tried to tell myself that maybe I should just come clean about the ordeal. You know, tell him of the plan that Do-Dirty, who was his baby mamma, and Jasmine her friend, along with some grimy ass nigga named Goldmouth had orchestrated how they all were going to rob me and my ladies of all the money we had stored up in our house. Even wanting to bust open my safe. Goosebumps crawled up my right arm as I relived that dreadful night inside my head.

Seconds later, I was like, "Nah. If I did that, greed might invade his simple-minded ass." Hell, he might even try to extort me, or better yet, try his hand at robbing me and the ladies as well. You can never underestimate another nigga in the streets. Shit, I had read a book one time where this brother had titled it. *Trust No Man.* Something we should practice every day. Maybe if I would have done that, I wouldn't be writing this book to tell my side of the story.

With all of that going on, I realized one thing that made sense to me. I should have never let his ass get next to me. I had to make a critical decision. One that just might come back to haunt my black ass later on down the road.

Just as those sentiments danced around my dome is when the silence turned into what sounded like angels humming all around me like the music was in Dolby surround sound. That's when he appeared, just like if I had called his smooth, debonair looking ass. Nigga was looking like his ass had just stepped out of a Jet Magazine. You know, like the Eddie Murphy edition. His lit Cuban Cigar hung slightly to the left side of his mouth. His head was held high enough so that I could see the nice tight circle pattern of the waves that he had adorned on top of his head. After I peeped the waves is when he then lifted his head lazily. He now stood a few feet in front of me.

"You know too many young brothers like ourselves are gone too soon. It's like someone has been praying for us, because we could have been six feet deep, laying somewhere in a box two feet wide." My eager looking face could only stare at my conscience as he stood there thinking of what he wanted to say since he was so gifted. Then his lips parted again. "I said all of that to say this. Sometimes we got to do what we got to in order to stay ahead of this mean game of life, that my friend the Devil seems to play for keeps. You know as well as I do that there are even some licks that our dear momma isn't proud of. But that's what we had to do in order to remain on top."

I then looked my conscience straight in his dark eyes and said, "So what are you saying?" I had a quizzical look glazed on my face.

Now his smirk turned into his sinister smile. "You know the one that I said in the first book that I copied from Prince in the hit movie Purple Rain? Yeah, that one. We got to do what we got to. In other words, my son. Cousin has to go. You will learn later on in life that you have to have love for those that hold you down no matter what. We can always replace the ones we love with someone else. Just be thankful." He licked his parched lips. "And remember this."

"What' s that?" I asked as I somberly looked at him with sincere in my moist eyes.

His face then held the most serious look on it that I had ever seen before. A side that I had never seen. "Like I said before, so take it to the heart, lil' ass nigga. Someone is always praying for us." He then spun on his heels, dressed from head to toe in an all black Armani suit. The brother even had on a nice pair of Stacey Addams that shined brightly in the light of my kitchen.

Walking away I could still hear those same angels humming once again as he walked with a slight pimp in his step. A pimp that I never even knew. "Hey, what happened to your leg?" I asked as he stopped at the corner of the foyer.

"Same thing that will happen to yours in your immediate future." He left cigar smoke as he pimp-walked away, leaving me behind to do what I had to do, if I wanted to stay ahead of the game. Not to mention stay free.

Oh, well. One thing for sure and two things for certain. I had females known as the Murder Queens to hold me down now.

# CHAPTER 70
## FINE AS HELL!

I stood still as I looked over at Richard and said, "You know, I keep saying the same thing myself Richard, but then I quickly put that notion out of my head."

"She's fucking beautiful Mike, so which one are you going to put the ring on?"

"I don't know Rich, but one of them will be my wife one day. Now about you, how is everything been going for you?" I then slapped him on his back, while ushering him back into the kitchen with the ladies.

"So, what are you going to do with that piece of chicken in your hands. Eat it or throw it away?"

"My bad Rhynyia, I'm definitely not going to eat it. Where is the trash can?"

"Oh yes you are, my boy. You don't throw nothing away around here," I replied with a stern voice, and serious look on my face.

He stood there puzzled for a brief minute, as if he wanted to say. 'For real cousin, you're going to make me eat this piece of chicken that I dropped on the floor?'

"Man, I'm just fucking with you. Here, let me throw this away for you." We all began laughing as Yani and Rhynyia walked out to the pool area to eat their food.

"Now, back to your question. Everything is everything," he said as he stood there searching for another giant piece of chicken.

"What in the hell does that mean?"

"Nothing man, nothing. I'm still high."

"High?"

"Yes, you know ever since your girl Chazz hooked me up with her supplier, my head has been in the clouds. And besides, I'm still dealing with the loss of my kids' mother."

"I guess you have a point, my bad, cousin."

Thirty minutes later, everyone was at the house, slowly entering into the meeting room. The ladies were a bit shocked to see that I was still home, but the excitement was when Rhynyia walked into the room.

Everyone was quiet as a mouse, when she took the floor for the meeting that I would always have with them before doing a show.

"PST, I thought she was in Puerto Rico," Suga Bear said as Rhynyia walked to the front of the room to address the room full of beautiful ladies.

"I don't care where she was, all I know is that she's fine as hell, Suga Bear," Peekachu uttered as Rhynyia sashayed past her, swaying her ass cheeks from side to side.

"Whatever Peekachu, and my name is not no damn Suga Bear."

"Whatever hoe, the bitch is bad. And Mike said that your damn name is Suga Bear, so Suga Bear, it is. Now be quiet and listen to the meeting. It might be something that you really need to hear."

# CHAPTER 71
## WELCOME BACK!

Forty five minutes later, Sexy Redd was finishing up the meeting. The females went to their different vehicles that they were riding in. On the way out of the house, one of Richard's girls walked up to me, and said, "Excuse me Mike, do we really have to go to Apollo South? Why can't we all just go over to Hollywood with the rest of the group?"

"Hey Rich, how many do you have that want to go to Apollo?"

"I don't know, but I can find out."

After a few minutes of him speaking with the females inside his truck, it was decided that everyone would go to Hollywood Nites.

A decision that I really didn't like, due to it meaning that I wasn't taking any females to the club that gave the Hot Girls their big break into the stripping industry.

The ride to Tampa started out quiet until Charlie B shouted from the back seat.

"Hey Sexy Redd, it's so good to finally have your ass back."

She turned her head to look in the back seat as she replied. "Yeah, it's good to be back, but I won't be here for too long."

"That's cool, just know that your fine ass has been missed. Welcome back!"

"Thank you, Charlie B, I have missed you girls as well."

"Girl, you should've been here a few weeks ago, when all the girls found out, who you are, and where you're from!"

"Believe me I heard. And for you ladies, who can't believe that I'm shaking my ass for some cash, come and ask me why I do what it is that I do!"

Everyone got quiet, as all eyes focused in on Lil' Kitty, who just turned up her mouth and turned to look out of the window, acting as if she wasn't even there.

After that, the girls all sat quiet to themselves as if they all had something else on their mind. No one even asked where Nicole was, nor did they ask why Strawberry had her arm wrapped up in a sling, sitting on a bag of ice. Due to her vagina being swollen, after my brother had broken her back in. She told me that her pussy would be out of commission for at least a few weeks, or so.

The entire time that we were on the road, all I could do was just sit there and laugh at the way she was sitting and frowning up her face, every time that my brother hit a bump in the highway.

When we finally got to the club, the mood was somewhat somber. For what reason I didn't know, but when all of the ladies walked into the club and heard the DJ playing Zoom by Boosie Bad Azz and Young Joe, they quickly snapped into the right mood for one of the hottest strip clubs on the west coast of Florida.

# CHAPTER 72
## CLOSE AND PERSONAL!

Now the DJ that played the music at Hollywood Nites, was this huge guy that called himself the Teddy Bear. He really knew how to get the club and the girls pumping. He was actually the guy who gave me the name Orlando Mike, a name that still sticks to me this very day.

After the very first night of us being there, I would be known as Orlando Mike, and the girls, of course, their name was the world-famous Florida Hot Girls.

The Teddy Bear had this smooth ass voice that resonated throughout the whole entire club. In other words, he always knew how to get the crowd in the right mood and keep smiles on the faces of the females that were dancing inside the club.

He kept the club jumping from start to finish every night that we were there.

Once all of the ladies came out of the small ass bathroom that the club had them use as their make shift dressing room, it was on. They all hit the floor like trained professional dancers.

I took my seat at the back of the club at the bar so that I could watch all of them at work. My girl Yani even put on a nice lil' outfit and actually danced out on the dance floor, making her some extra cash.

Richard and Firstborn joined me at the bar, watching everyone that came in through the door. The word had gotten out that it was new girls coming in every Tuesday night from all over. Heads immediately snapped around when we heard Teddy Bear come over the speaker system with.

"Ladies and gentlemen, cats and dogs, please get your money right, for the beautiful Sexy Redd and Mignon! Members of the gorgeous women that came in with Orlando Mike! They are from the sensual, sexy, tantalizing group of bad ass women, known as the world famous, Florida Hot Girls!"

Both came out on stage looking like a million bucks. Some people actually thought that they were sisters, as fine as they looked on stage.

I just couldn't help but think to myself what my life would be like without Sexy Redd or the Hot Girls in it, as she danced on stage, and the ladies all around the club.

While they danced on stage, Chyna and a few of the other girls were over at the picture booth, taking pictures with every guy who wanted one with them.

Chazz was in the back of the club dancing on some guy, who had a head full of dreads, while smoking on some good ass weed. It was so good that she would later on that night leave the club with the guy, because his weed so good.

Her baby sister, Suga Bear, was hugged up with her good friend Busta, while her girl Peekachu still walked around the club with her two dollar thong, pulled up in the crack of her ass so far, that you couldn't even see it. It looked like she had on nothing at all. One of the managers had been by the bar area twice already, saying to me. "Hey Mike, the girls are not permitted to walk around the club naked."

"I know, she's not naked. Her cheap ass thong is just pulled all up in the crack of her lil' red ass. You are welcome to go pull it out with your teeth if you like."

"Nah, I don't think so partner. Just make sure she has on some proper clothing the next time you guys are here."

"Yes sir, boss," I replied, as I continued smiling and sipping at the same time.

Your girl Lil' Kitty, had the number of the guy in the wheel chair, so she called him earlier that day and let him and his driver know that we would be in town, so that she could take the rest of the poor guys damn social security check. It seemed like Lil' Kitty always would have someone's damn number and call them to alert them that we would be coming to their spot. That Damn Lil' Hot Ass Lil' Kitty.

Now Charlie Band, her lil' waitress friend, were both standing over by the DJ booth, sipping on some drinks, before they got drunk. My favorite girl Yani, had like four guys all around her, as she showed them what an Island girls vagina looked like, up close and personal.

# CHAPTER 73
## LAST TIME TOGETHER!

As the night dragged on, I still couldn't forget what I had went through earlier that morning. The constant thought of how everything went down was still fresh on my mind.

First, it was the mere thought of how Sharon and my unborn child were doing. I didn't know if she had gained consciousness yet, or had she woke up and wanted to see me.

Then, it was the image of Nicole dancing in my head. I hadn't had a chance to speak to her since the doctors and nurses ran inside her room, once she awoke. I was so distraught that I guess I would have to speak to her once I reached back home from Puerto Rico.

As I sat there pondering those thoughts in my head, Firstborn and Richard sat next to me conversating with one another, with us not knowing that this would be our last night together, as the guys who had all those bad ass females with them.

My brother and I were about to embark on a trip to Puerto Rico, while dear Richard would be left behind to run the squad, until our return. Mignon and Entyce would help Richard, with the daily operations of the group, hoping that I still had a group, when I got back.

As I sat there watching those two laugh it up over drinks and half butt naked women, crawling over us, while we sat there. My mind definitely drifted somewhere else. It wasn't until Sexy Redd walked off stage after her set and wrapped her arm around my neck, while placing her soft ass on my lap.

"What's wrong, Papi, you look like your head is somewhere else?"

"Nothing baby girl, just thinking about are trip tomorrow. That's all," I said to her, while turning my head, to look directly into those big pretty brown eyes of hers. And at the same time, grabbing me a handful of her soft caramel ass.

"Alright, you're going to get something started up in here, and you and I both know that we can't finish it up in here," she whispered, while laughing in my ear.

"Nah, I'm going to wait until I get you back home before I do that."

As we both sat there laughing at my comment, Firstborn and Richard decided to take a stroll around the club, to check on the girls. They had just walked up on the first set of stairs, when Richard turned to him and said. "Man, it's some fine ass women up in here tonight."

"Yes it is my boy. I must admit that there are quite a few. But all I see is my lil' boo thang, Strawberry," Firstborn recited, as Richard looked over at him and said.

"So you're the nigga that has her pussy all swollen?"

"Yep, she told me that you were trying to wife her ass, but I had to show her how big cuzz be putting in work," Firstborn said to Richard, while grabbing his crotch and smiling.

"Whatever cuzz."

"For real, watch this." Firstborn then yelled across the dance floor out to Strawberry. When she looked back at him, he grabbed his crotch area again, causing her to point down to her swollen pussy and look back up with a nasty ass frown on her face.

Him and Richard burst into laughter, as he spilled his ten dollar glass of Cognac on the floor.

"Damn nigga, your drunk ass spilling shit everywhere!"

"It don't matter nigga, watch this." Firstborn then waved over to one of the waitresses, and ordered another glass.

"I'm 'bout to get so fucked up in here, that I won't wake up until we get to Puerto Rico, tomorrow," he said to Richard, while barely being able to get his drink from the waitress.

# CHAPTER 74
### FULL BENEFITS!

Both were still standing, talking and laughing amongst one another, when one of the local dancers walked up and asked them. "Excuse me, do you guys want a dance?"

Richard cut a wicked smile her way as he stepped back to get a good look at the short, gorgeous looking, light skinned dancer, while grabbing at his dick, and said. "Hell yeah ma, you're fine as hell!"

The very cute young lady began slow grinding on Richards manhood, as my drunk ass brother started dancing in front of her, while holding his drink up in the air, screaming, and yelling. "Madville, where you at baby?" knowing goddamn well, that there was nobody from no country ass Madison, Florida, up in the club. And if they were, they sure as hell was not about to let anyone know it.

No one would know about Madison, Florida until my brother and Pierre Santiago, got together and started running so much product through that small ass town, that they would have to come up with another name for what he was trafficking, from one end of the map, to the other.

***

Meanwhile, as Chief Jones sat back in his favorite chair inside his plush office, and witnessed what the beautiful reporter, Tasha Willis was reporting on. He could only put his head down, due to him wanting to keep the incident quiet until he could put a lid on it.

He then placed his hands over his nicely shaven bald head and realized the aftermath that was about to ensue would literally cause him to resign his position within the force after the entire city knew of the corrupt cops plan to kidnap a local woman over the money that the force had to pay her family for killing one of her relatives.

Which was made to seem, after I had leaked the incident to the right sources, so no one besides the police department would know about the two hundred and fifty thousand dollars that went missing from the evidence room of the police department. The local media had a field day, and swarmed the police station as soon as the report went out over the news that early Wednesday morning. Chief Jones could only wait until his world as he knew it all caved in on top of him. There was nothing that he could do about it.

First, it was the Mayor, who called him and wanted to know what type of operation he was running. Then, it was the city advisors, asking for his head on a silver platter. Chief Jones' stellar reputation and career was now being tarnished, not only by his peers, but by the citizens of Orlando.

He had been transferred to the department from the Medulla Police Department to help rationalize the problem that the police force had within their ranks. But now that this new form of behavior had surfaced and influenced some of its senior personnel, he was left baffled at what had become of his engrossed department.

The city advisors felt as though he had lost control of his department, and once they came down on the Mayor, the only choice left for Chief Jones was for him to resign his position with full benefits.

# CHAPTER 75
## TANTALIZING!

It was almost noon when I received the call that would kick off my busy day. Rhynyia and I were fast asleep when the phone began ringing off of the hook. We all had only been back from Tampa for a few hours when I finally rolled over to answer my phone.

"Hello," I answered, sounding half awake.

"Michael, is this you?" the mild mannered sexy voice on the other end asked me.

By the romantic, soothing sound of the young temptress on the other end, I knew that it could be no one other than the attractive looking, Tasha Willis, from Channel Eleven news.

"Yes."

"I didn't mean to wake you. The world knows how important and busy you are."

I eased up in bed, placing a pillow behind my back and then said. "Flattery gets you nowhere, beautiful. Now, what's on your eager mind, young lady?"

"I was just calling to inform you of the disposition that was becoming at your local police department, downtown."

"The what?"

"Turn your television on the news, Mr. Vallentino, and have a nice time down in Puerto Rico."

At first I smiled, and then I was like, "Hey, wait a minute, how do you know about my trip down to Puerto Rico?"

203

"Mr. Vallentino, should I remind you that's what I do. I find out the news on what goes on. Now turn on your television before it's too late. And oh, before I forget, thank you once again for the scoop."

"You're welcome. You have a nice day as well." I hung up, searching the night stand for the remote.

Just as I found it, I flipped to the news, to see. "This is Brandon Moore, reporting live from police headquarters, with breaking news of what looks like the resignation of embattled police Chief, Trevor Jones.

The Chief has been under fire since the news broke out of the corrupt police officers with in his department."

I turned over in my bed, trying not to disturb Rhynyia, watching the entire broadcast of a good police officer's brilliant career, tarnished by a few bad cops, that he had on his force.

I wanted to scream at the television as this man of fifteen years or so, had dedicated his entire life for something he believed in. And then have it all stripped away because of a few bad apples in his department.

It wasn't his fault that those cops all decided to use their badge and power to do things their way and not the official way. If only there was some way that I could give the Chief just what he needed to clear his name of their mistakes and wrong doings.

As I laid there in my bed thinking to myself, I knew what it was that I had to do, but it would all have to wait until I had returned back home from Puerto Rico.

I numbly turned my head to see the time on the clock on the wall, which displayed twelve forty two, and our flight left at two, that afternoon. We would drop Yani off in Miami, and then fly on to Puerto Rico, landing at the San Juan International Airport.

As I got up and headed for the shower, Rhynyia rolled her naked body over, and continued to lay there fast asleep, or that's what I thought at least.

As I stood there in the door way, for a minute or two, yearning and lusting for her naked body, it dawned on me that we had just made love hours ago when we arrived home.

It was just something about the way her warm vagina wrapped around my manhood. The sensation drove me wild and had me craving for more as she laid there pretending to be sleep.

Now that she was caring her first child, her womb felt so warm as my manhood loved the way she would tighten up her muscles and make her womb, just that more tantalizing.

# CHAPTER 76
## STRIKING RESEMBLANCE!

I quickly erased the thought of having hot passionate sex with her, as I jumped my naked body inside my hot steamy shower, and cleansed myself. While standing there with the hot water pulsating off of my back, I could only wonder what may lay ahead for me in the next chapter of my extraordinary life.

I stepped back and started washing over my chest, when Sexy Redd snuck her gorgeous looking, naked body into the shower with me. Her breath still smelt of the waffles and steak that she had for breakfast, as she said, "Good morning Michael."

"Good morning to you also, pretty lady," I replied, as my manhood began to transform, right before her very eyes.

"Wow, I guess something else must be up to, huh?"

"I guess so baby." She then turned and placed her ass cheeks up against my hardened manhood, while I started massaging her soft, tender stomach, with my left hand.

I then took my right hand and gently inserted my manhood up inside her from the back. She instantly bent over, allowing me to place all ten and a half inches of rock hard dick inside her.

Once she had all of me inside her, she slowly began moving back and forth, while pushing my back up against the wall.

With the pulsating water hitting her in the small of her back, and then bouncing back up against my chest, she turned to look me in the face and said. "I want you to cum all over my back, baby."

"Whatever you say baby."

\*\*\*

An hour later, we were both in the bedroom putting on our attire for the day. She was standing at the mirror brushing her hair when she looked over at me walking out of the closet.

"Michael, the weather down in Puerto Rico is nice and warm around this time of year. So please dress casual honey."

I had chosen a few outfits to wear while I was there, but I knew that we would probably do some shopping. I didn't want to pack too much. She stood there still brushing her hair, with nothing on but her thong and a nice bra to cover up her nice size breasts. I slid on a nice pair of white slacks, with an orange silk Versace shirt to go along with my outfit. As soon as I slid on my orange colored Stacey Adams, and pranced across the floor, I knew I was about to hear her mouth.

"Damn boy, you love them damn Stacey Adams, don't you?"

I sat on the edge of the bed, smiling back at her and said. "Yes, and what is wrong with my Stacey Adams?"

"Nothing, but why can't you wear some Jordans or something?"

"Whatever. I'm not about to be playing no damn basketball, so why do I need on some damn basketball shoes," I replied, as I stood up to look at myself in the full length mirror.

"Okay Michael, you and my father kill me with the way y'all be dressing." she voiced as she slid on a nice pair of knee high channel silk pants, along with a nice, assorted color halter top.

She topped her outfit off with some cute comfortable looking white sandals and a pair of Gucci shades to cover her elegant looking eyes.

"Okay Michael, do we have everything?"

"Yes, I packed light as possible, sweetheart."

"Yeah, me too." she recited as we both walked out of the room, headed to the stairs.

While walking downstairs, the girls met us at the door way of the kitchen, all with something to drink off in their hand.

"Oh, so you two were just going to leave without saying goodbye?" Mignon said as the rest of them sipped on something nice and fruity from their cups.

"Nah chick, you know I had to come find my girls so I could say goodbye. Where is the one new chick, Tameia?"

"Right here, Redd!" Tameia shouted from the guest room down the hall.

"I was just about to come find you and Michael before you guys left." She recited, with a strange look on her face.

"What's wrong, Tameia? You look like something is wrong?"

"It just might be, Michael. I guess you all haven't seen the twelve o'clock news?"

She had the entire room's attention as I looked at her and uttered. "Yes, I seen where the Chief announced his retirement."

She brashly began shaking her head as she fixed her mouth to say. "Nah, that's not it. They say that the witness they had at the shooting at Red Lobster has identified the women who did the shooting."

"What?"

"Mike, they had a sketch artist flown in from New York. The pictures that he drew have a striking resemblance to—"

# CHAPTER 77
## ALL BE MURDER QUEENS!

Just as the words rolled off of her small ass lips, I felt that sinking feeling all over again. I stared hard and very long at her, when I asked her. "Who did the pictures look like?"

She pokily looked back up at me, and then pointed at Strawberry, Entyce, and of course, the damn Mastermind of the flawless plan, Mignon.

"Damn, I knew something like this would eventually happen. Fuck, what are we to do now?" I yelled as Rhynyia casually put her bags down.

"Michael, get a grip. Everything is going to be okay."

"Excuse me, but what is going on? Is it true? Are you the females that shot up that Red Lobster?"

Mignon informally smiled back at Tameia, and then recited. "Why of course not, my young friend. There has to be some kind of mistake. Don't worry yourself. Now, go on back to whatever it was that you were doing, while I try to make some type of sense out of this small simple matter."

"Okay," Tameia replied, as she turned and walked back to her room.

***

Meanwhile, I was out at the pool area, with Rhynyia, Entyce and Strawberry. I was standing looking out over the pool, wondering what would be my next move. The Murder

Queens had been there for me, now it was my turn to be there for them.

"So, I guess we cancel the flight for right now?"

"Hell nah, Michael, you must have forgot, I'm the bitch who runs that. Now calm down for a second while we all put our heads together and work this thing out."

"No need for that, Rhynyia. You guys go ahead and make your flight. The ladies and I will handle the rest."

"What are you talking about Entyce? How? Didn't you just hear what Tameia said?"

"Yes I did, Mike. But what you all don't know is that I have that bitch's ID."

"What?" I yelped while turning to face Entyce.

"Her ID. It's inside Nicole's glove compartment. The girls and I will pay her young naive ass a visit. When we get through talking with her ass, she will have a slight case of amnesia!"

"So, you're telling me that you guys got this?"

"Yes Mike, trust me. Now go ahead and get to the airport. The ladies and I have a lil trip to take ourselves."

I cut a wicked evil grin back at her when Mignon emerged from out of the house.

"So, what's the plan, Rhynyia?"

"It seems as though your girl Entyce has the plan already."

"How?" Mignon uttered, as she turned to look at Entyce.

"Don't worry chick. I got this. Remember when I was inside watching Nicole."

"Yes. Go on."

"The waitress, who worked her booth, that's who the police have as a witness."

"Okay, so what?"

"I have the bitch's ID, Mignon, duh."

"Oh."

"But hold on Entyce. The police are going to have security up the ass for this lil snitching ass bitch."

"That might be true Rhynyia, but you forget one thing."

"What's that girl?"

"We're the Murder Queens. We have everything covered. Now like I said, you guys go ahead and catch your flight. The ladies and I have a lil trip of our own to plan. We have the next few days off, so we'll be busy handling our lil problem."

"What about Tameia? Do you think she suspects anything?"

"I have no idea, Mike, I talked to her for a lil bit. We'll just have to play things by ear."

"If anything Mignon, put her on the team."

"Damn, before it's said and done, half of the squad of ladies that we have living with us will all be fucking Murder Queens."

# CHAPTER 78
## TIME WOULD TELL!

Rhynyia and I walked back through the house, grabbing our bags. We got to the garage to find Firstborn already inside the limo sleep behind the wheel. We must have startled him when he jumped up with saliva drooling down his face.

"Well I'll be. The house could have burned down, and your black ass would have never known it."

"What do you mean lil' bro?"

"Nothing man, do you have all your things packed and in the car?"

"Yes, I must've fell asleep out here waiting on y'all slow ass."

"Yes, you must have. Sorry for making you wait Firstborn, but we had a lil matter to handle before we left. Where's Yani?"

"I don't know. I thought that she was with you guys."

"Hold on, I'll get her."

Just as I turned to walk back into the house, she ran out to the garage, yelling.

"Me so sorry, I must have overslept. Last night was a trip."

"Yes it was. Let me have your bags. Go ahead and grab a seat. I was just about to come get you."

"Tanks, Michael."

"Don't mention it." she eased herself in, speaking to Rhynyia, as soon as she saw her bright beaming face.

"Hey girl, so sorry, dat I late. Must hab ober slept."

"It's okay girl, it happens. The plane doesn't leave without me anyway. Did you enjoy yourself while you were here?"

"Yes me did, I can't wait until I am needed again."

"Hopefully, we won't have to kill anyone any time soon," I said as I smiled at her.

"To the airport bro. Are you okay to drive?"

"Yeah man, sit back and relax!" He yelled as he hit the button, causing the garage door to rise.

It was around one fifteen as he slowly pulled out of the garage, just missing side swiping Entyce, who had her ass sticking out of Nicole's passenger door.

"Damn, I almost hit ole girl."

"Yep, you surly did."

"Shut up, Mike. Let your brother drive. Nicole has a nice lil bucket, I see."

"Whatever Rhynyia, trying to be funny. You know everybody can't afford luxury like some of us can."

"I was not trying to be funny, for real. I like her little car."

"Yeah, all I was saying is that he almost took off the hip of ole Entyce."

"Almost, but he didn't. Now lay back and get some rest."

"Thanks."

I laid my head back, wishing that someone would have told me what lay ahead for my brother and I, before we boarded that private G-4 headed for Puerto Rico.

Since we were pressed for time, we didn't have a chance to go by and check on Nicole or Sharon. I knew both would be heartbroken, when they realized that I had left without saying goodbye.

I never liked saying goodbye, because goodbye meant forever, and Yahweh knew, I was praying that I came back. To what? Only time would tell.

# CHAPTER 79
## YES!

As Firstborn pulled the limo into the hangar that we would leave our limo in, I thought to myself about what was waiting for us, once we got to Puerto Rico, and what should I expect from Rhynyia's father, the infamous Pierre Santiago.

As we all got out, waiting to climb aboard the private G-4, that was there waiting for our arrival. Poor Rhynyia had the look of a young kid, off to their very first day of school on her face, with the way she was smiling from ear to ear.

Yani, slept all the way to the airport, due to her not being used to staying out all night, shaking her ass for a little cash. Firstborn, somehow got us to the airport safely, even though his ass was still partially drunk from last night.

Me, on the other hand, was looking around to see if the cops were going to be after us again, like the previous time. But after I stood there, taking in everything, I figured that the coast was clear.

The ladies boarded the plane first, while Firstborn and myself waited until they got half way up the stairs to the plane. As I stood there staring at his attire, I was like. "Man, what in the hell do you have on?"

He looked down at his mix matched shoes and realized that he had on two different pair of sneakers, along with a pair of wrinkled up shorts. Not to mention a torn up Michael Jordan jersey covering up his chest.

"Ah man, I'm still drunk, and besides, we about to go down to Puerto Rico. Ain't we going shopping once we get there?" he asked, while trying to keep his balance.

"Hey man, don't get that ass down here and embarrass us, please." I muttered, as I walked up the flight of stairs, trying to leave his non dressing ass behind me.

"Good afternoon, Senor Vallentino," Maria said to me as she reached out for my luggage, and placed it inside one of the storage compartments.

"Good afternoon to you as well, Maria."

Rhynyia was already seated as she gingerly placed her seatbelt tenderly around her bulging tummy.

Baby, I want you sitting next to me, not across from me," she said as Firstborn, fell his drunk ass down onto the couch, and then pulled his hat over his red eyes.

"Y'all be so kind as to wake my ass up when we get to Puerto Rico." he then threw up two fingers, as though he was trying to say peace.

Yani, who grabbed her a nice comfortable seat in the back, placed her shades over her eyes and followed suit, as to what Firstborn had just did.

Minutes later, the private luxury jet was taking off, headed for San Juan, Puerto Rico. I glanced over to the right, looking out of the window of the exquisite looking plane. It rolled down the runway, about to ascend up into the heavens and away from the hustle and bustle of my surroundings.

While Rhynyia adjusted her blinders that she had placed over her eyes, she gently leaned over, placing her head on my shoulders. She whispered softly into my ear. "I love you Michael Vallentino, and so does your baby." She then motioned for me to give her a kiss.

As I kissed her soft tender lips, I replied. "I love you more, Rhynyia Marisa Vallentino." she smiled as she said.

"Rhynyia Vallentino. Yes, that does sound nice to my ears. When do we make that official?"

Just as soon as you take those ugly ass blinders off."

She frantically snatched them off to see the nice ten thousand dollar engagement ring that I had purchased for her.

Her eyes grew as large as her breast, as tears of joy jumped out of her eyes. I then got down on one knee and said. "I was going to wait until we all arrived in Puerto Rico, but why put off today, for tomorrow. Rhynyia Marisa Santiago, will you marry me?" I gently slid the ring on her finger, as she desperately tried to fight back her tears of joy that wouldn't stop flowing down her face.

"Michael, I've been waiting on this day, ever since the moment I first laid eyes on your sexy black ass inside that damn Winn Dixie grocery store in Pine Hills. Of course I will! Yesssssssssss, I'll marry you!"

# CHAPTER 80
## TO US!

Rhynyia and the rest of us had been gone for only a few hours, when the girls found themselves in a pickle. They didn't know whom their witness was, nor where she lived.

"Entyce, hey, let me holla at cha for a minute!" Mignon yelled when she saw Entyce walk back in through the garage door.

"Yeah, what's up chick?" she said as she walked up on Mignon, who stood in the door way of the foyer with a quizzical look on her face.

"The witness, you say that you have her ID, right?"

"Mignon, it's right here," Entyce said as she took the ID from her pocket to show Mignon.

"Here, let me see that." Mignon then took the ID.

Minutes went by as she stood there contemplating, then looking back up at Entyce, who stood firm as she folded her arms, waiting on Mignon to say something.

"Strawberry, do you remember seeing this lady at that Red Lobster?"

"Here, let me see that," she said as she nudged in behind Mignon to get a good a better look at the picture ID.

"Nah, I don't remember her," Strawberry said, as she shook her head.

"Precisely. This is not the woman who is talking to the police."

"What do you mean, Mignon. I took the girls ID who saw me."

"I know that Entyce. But this bitch wasn't the one who saw all four of us in the rest room, remember?"

"Oh snap, your absolutely right. It was the one lil short bitch who shitted on us!"

"Your damn right. Now we have a bigger problem than I thought."

"Why?"

"Strawberry, how do we find that hoe? Hell, we have the ID of the female who saw Entyce. And most likely she knows that Entyce has her ID, so she's not our problem. The one who saw all of us, is the one who I bet is doing the talking. Especially since them crackers have a hundred thousand dollar reward out on our fucking heads!"

"A hundred k?"

"Yes Strawberry. A hundred k," Mignon muttered, causing her lips to turn to the left side of her mouth, looking like Bobby Brown, after a good taste of what he liked the most.

"Damn, they want us bad, don't they?"

"Yep. Dead or alive! Entyce. Dead or alive," Mignon replied as she turned her head in disgust.

"Damn! I don't think that I'm ready to die yet." "Neither are we Berry. Neither are we." Entyce voiced, while looking away, with serious doubt in her mind.

"So we do have a problem?" Strawberry recited sarcastically, as she looked back over at Mignon.

"Yep, we all do."

"She's right, Strawberry."

"I know I am, Entyce. Now how do we find the bitch that we really need to get at?" Mignon asked, as she took a glass out of the dishwasher, then searched for something to drink.

The ladies all stood motionless, looking around at one another, as if they were looking for answers to fall from the sky.

It wasn't until Entyce snapped her fingers and came back at them with.

"Hey, wait just a minute. I know what we can do," she said as her head went up and down slowly, revealing an alarming smile on her face.

"What?"

"Mignon, we have the ID right?"

"Yes."

"Okay, we go back to the Red Lobster, get with this one female, that ID I took!"

"For what?"

"So she can check the cameras, for the one chick who saw our faces."

"Entyce, we still have to be there. How is she going to know which chick to look for?"

"She's right, Entyce."

"I know that Berry. Shut up, let me finish. We have to go back to the restaurant, wait until they close, and run up in that bitch with our face covered. Take the manager and whomever else is still there, and then, we check the footage for ourselves. Once we see her face, we'll know who she is. Hopefully the bitch paid with her credit card. Get her name, and then we find her address."

"What if she paid with cash?"

"What if she didn't Mignon?"

"She's right, Mignon. It's worth a try. And by the way, how in the hell do you know it's a hundred thousand dollar reward out for us?"

"I didn't. It wasn't until I saw what Tameia saw on TV."

"So, wait a fucking minute! You knew about the reward, and didn't say anything?" Strawberry asked with a shrug smirk across her face.

"Yes Strawberry. I didn't want Mike to find out. Shit, he already has enough to deal with. I guess you all didn't know that he was given an order to kill Nicole?"

"What? When?"

"Yesterday."

"By who? Who would want one of us dead, besides the niggas in Jacksonville?" Entyce asked, as she stood there with an uncertain look on her face.

"Think about it ladies. Who's man was she fucking?"

"Rhynyia." Entyce whispered out loud.

"Yep, Rhynyia."

"So, what happened? Did he do it?" Entyce asked.

"No, please don't tell me that his black ass went and killed her, and then got on a plane acting like nothing never happened!" Strawberry yelled as she went for the door, leading out to the pool area.

"No, Entyce. He didn't. He couldn't kill her, even if he tried. Not even if Nicole had a gun pointed at him. The poor man loves her too much. And besides, she saved his life."

"So, what did Rhynyia have to say about that?" Strawberry asked as she took a deep sigh, turning back around, but still worried about her friend Nicole.

"Once I explained to her how she stepped in and saved his life that night in St. Pete, she had a change of heart."

"I see. Okay, so since she's still alive, let's go see our girl." Entyce sputtered, as a smile ran across her face.

"Sounds good to me. We go see her, but first, we have to check and see if this bitch is working today. If so, we see Nicole, and then we have to go back to Daytona. We have to get to the snitch before they get to us!" Mignon remarked, as she reached for the cordless phone.

# CHAPTER 81
## THE GIRL!

Yes, that's right. I proposed to Rhynyia Marisa Santiago. I know that you're probably saying.

'Oh no, what about Sharon, or even poor banged up Nicole?'

Believe me when I tell you all, I thought about all the different scenarios, weighed all of my options but only one stood out to me. And that was my girl Rhynyia. Hell, it was the most profitable scenario for me to adjust to enjoy, in the prime of my complicated life. Her and her family were loaded! I would become a Hood Millionaire overnight.

She marveled at the enormous size of the rock on her outstretched hand, and with the sheer excitement of being my wife. She just couldn't stop the tears from streaming down her face.

Yani stood to her feet to stare at the massive size ring that I had purchased for Rhynyia, as she looked at her and said. "C, I told yo' ass dat he truly lubed u!" Rhynyia stood to embrace Yani, when she replied with. "Girl, I guess you were right!"

"So when is de lucky day, and am I ind wedding, Rhynyia?"

"Yes, of course you are. I wouldn't have it any other way," Rhynyia remarked in excitement .

\*\*\*

Back in Orlando, Florida. Sharon was just rolling over in bed to find her mother sitting next to her bedside, waiting on her to wake up.

"Hey mom, what are you doing here, and where is Michael and Breanna?" she asked her mother, sounding still half sleep, and tired.

Her mother reached out for her daughter's weak hand, and then uttered. "I'm here because you're my daughter and I was worried sick about you. The question about where your Prince Charming is. I have no earthly idea. I haven't seen him since the night that they rescued you.

He must've been by to see you though because here are some flowers, with a card attached to them, with his name attached to them. Now the answer to the question about your lil one, is that she's at your aunt's house, playing with all of the other kids."

"The flowers are beautiful. But I told his ass that I wanted him here with me when I spoke to him."

"Like I said baby, maybe he was, but you know he stays busy. And I know you don't know this, but one of the young ladies that work with him, arrived around the same time that you arrived."

"Oh, do you know which one it was?"

"No, he didn't say. But I think her last name was Jackson, or something like that."

"Okay, well I guess he'll get to me when he has a chance."

"I know he will baby. Now, how are you feeling?"

"I'm fine mother, just a bit tired, and sore," she recited as she reached for a glass of water to quench her thirst.

After she swallowed a few sips of the refreshing cold water, she eased back and looked at her mother, and said. "Mom, you're not going to believe who it was that kidnapped me and Breanna."

"I do know that it was some crooked cops, because we saw it on the news."

"What happened? Did they catch them? The last thing I remember is being placed in the back seat of Michael's truck, amidst all of the gunfire."

"I know it had to be traumatizing to you."

"Yes ma'am, and if I wouldn't have been quick on my feet, Breanna and I would probably still be there inside that small ass room!"

"Thank God that you were able to get away."

"Yes, right along with Michael and some of the girls that works with him. You won't believe the gun battle that ensued," she said as she eased back down in her bed, grimacing, due to the severe pain in her back.

"Was anyone else hurt?"

"I don't know ma. All I know is that Michael had his brother bring me here. That's all I can remember. Wait a minute, the girl that I laid my head on. I think that I've seen her face before."

"Take it easy baby, you need to rest."

"No ma. The girl, I know that I've seen her face before I just can't remember where!" she said, as she slowly dozed back off to sleep."

"Sharon, Sharon baby, are you alright?" her mother asked, just as she heard a shy knock at her daughters hospital door.

# CHAPTER 82
## LEFT ALONE FOR THE WEEKEND!

In lovely Jacksonville, Florida, the news of the deadly assailant, who had been gun downed by the Murder Queens, wasn't taken to well by the man who sent him. Revenge and death were brewing heavy on the mind of the man responsible for sending death their way.

"So, do you know when the next time them hoes will be back in town, Punkin?" Marquise asked his Do-Boy, who just happened to be one of the guys who had had their way with Strawberry the morning that they had sent her back with no money, and a wet ass, and pussy.

"Not really, but all I have to do is call this one lil short female in their group, put a lil sugar on the treat, to get her to convince ole boy to drive them up for the weekend." he voiced as he sat back, thinking of what to say.

"Here, make the call! I can't wait to get my hands on them bitches that killed my baby brother! Not to mention his cousin and his love sick dumb ass! I told that nigga that them hoes were deadly!" Marquise voiced, as he handed Punkin his burner cell phone.

Marquise was thirty eight hot. Livid, that his lone gunman had been killed, trying to avenge his little brother's murder. Once he got the awful news, he vowed to kill everyone that was associated with the demise of his close friend and brother.

The huge beast of a man stood six foot four, weighing about two hundred and seventy five pounds. Big black, hard on the eyes looking brother, who looked as if he had just started growing dreads, due to him being in the ugly stage of the growth process. What people didn't realize, the brother, looked that way, all of the damn time.

His partial beer belly that hung off of his belt along with his very deep dark skinned complexion, kept the brother from getting the top notch females that resided in Duval County. Which meant he would always relish on the females that came into town to dance at the local strip clubs.

The massive being of a man, sleepily laid back in his chair, located inside his office, at the Barbecue joint he owned. It was located right down the road from Black Magic on Beaver Street. He stared down Punkin as he took the number out of his cell phone, and dialed the number of the one girl on my team, who just couldn't stop giving out her damn phone number, every time we went out of town.

A no-no, that I would always tell the females, due to them not knowing what the guy's intentions might have been for them. Now that she had made the ultimate mistake, not only were the Murder Queens put in a nasty situation, but the entire team as well. Now all of them would be left alone for the weekend.

# CHAPTER 83
### FYE BOTH HEADS UP!

Now the lil flunky Punkin, stood five foot seven, weighing a measly hundred and thirty five pounds soaking wet, with a dark brown skin complexion. He wore a very thin lined mustache to help cover up his wide narrow, skinny ass mouth.

Along the bottom of his mouth, he adorned a full set of gold teeth, that he would gladly show off every time he opened his narrow ass mouth, to smile, or talk. On top of his very small pea shaped head, was a well-kept Philly Fade haircut, that he would get done precisely at ten o'clock, every weekend. His fair looking girlfriend of three years, by the name of Sasha, would always tell his ass.

*'Punkin, if anyone ever wanted to kill you, all they would have to do, is be at that damn Barber shop every Saturday morning at ten o'clock sharp!'*

Needless to say, he never took her advice. Which would one day very soon be the benefit, of a group of ladies, called the Murder Queens when they got wind of his involvement with his partner Marquise.

The phone rang two times as the smooth sultry voice of the slim petite female of the Florida Hot Girls said, "Hello."

"Hey boo, what cha doing?"

"Nothing, what's good? Is this Punkin?" she politely asked.

"Yes. How did you know it was me boo?" he asked as he smiled back into the phone, revealing his gold teeth.

"Because I can hear you smiling, showing off them sexy ass golds. That's why. Now what's up, you about to come pick me up?" she asked, as she sat back on her bed smiling, hoping that he would say yes.

"Something like that. Hey, are you guys coming up this weekend because we really need to hook up."

"I don't know right now. Michael just left to go out of town. So that means his cousin is in charge of the group." she voiced, as she sat twirling her hair.

"Well me and a few of the homies want to spend some bread with y'all females this weekend. What's good?" he barked, placing the phone on speaker, so that Marquise could hear their conversation.

"That's what's up. Let me tell the girls, so Richard won't have no choice but to bring us up there this weekend."

"Alright, find out what's up and then hit me back on my phone when you find out."

"Okay, I'm 'bout to call Richard's ass right now, then I'm gonna hit a few of the girls. Stay by your phone, I'll call you right back."

They hung up, as the young hot tender female on my damn team did exactly what she said she would do.

When Richard seen that it was her on the phone, he answered on the first ring. "Hey, what's good, Lil' Kitty?"

"Nothing, hey listen. I just got a call from this guy from Jacksonville. He claims that him and his homies want to break bread with us this weekend."

Richard slowly slid the blunt that he was smoking on over to the ashtray in his truck, and then said. "Kitty, I don't know about that. You know how Mike doesn't like for you girls to give out your numbers, and now you have this guy calling you because you gave him your number."

"I know, but hell, his black ass is out of town, and the rest of us have bills to pay. While his ass is off in Puerto Rico, living it up."

"Damn Lil' Kitty, I thought you lived with your grandma, so what bills you paying, living in the projects?" he asked as he picked up his blunt.

"Whatever, it don't matter where I live. Me and the girls still need to make our bread! And besides, I have to pay my weed man!"

"I understand Lil' Kitty, but with what happened to them guys the other weekend, it might be best for us not to go up there. Lord knows I would hate for something to happen to one of y'all and I'm the one left holding the bag."

"Whatever man, it's gonna be some bread up there and we don't have anywhere else to dance this weekend. And fuck what happened to them dudes. Who ever got their ass, got 'em. Our girls are good. Hell, none of us hit them niggas anyway!" she angrily recited, while rolling her hot ass, a fat, thick ass, blunt.

"Tell you what. Let me call Mignon, and I'll get back with you, before this weekend."

"No, I need to know today, and soon, so I can have the nigga to pay for our rooms!"

"Gotcha, let me make the call," he muttered, as he choked on his blunt.

"Hey, sounds like your smoking," she said, smiling as she jumped up off of her bed, placing her weed down on her dresser.

"Yep." he uttered, while trying not to laugh.

"Damn nigga, come fye my head up. Then, you can tell me face to face. After that, I'll fye up, both of yo' heads!"

"Damn, say no more Lil' Kitty. I'm on my muthafucking way."

# CHAPTER 84
## WHISKED AWAY!

Now that's exactly why I didn't like for the ladies to give out their number to the guys out of town, either share their numbers between each other. She did just what she said she would do, the lil naive young tender called half of the crew of young ladies, and told them of what she was told by Punkin. It had all of them wanting to go to Jacksonville for the weekend. With neither of them knowing what lay ahead for them, and the Notorious Murder Queens, who had just pulled into the parking lot of the hospital, to check on one of their dear friends.

"Okay, listen real close you two. We go in, speak with our girl for a few minutes, then we break for Daytona." Mignon muttered as, she spoke to her two woman crew.

"No problem chick. Let's move. I miss my girl already."

"Hold up Entyce, let me get this damn sling off of my damn arm."

"Come here girl, let me help you with that." Just as Mignon reached over the seat to help Strawberry take off her sling, she heard her phone ringing.

"Damn Entyce, help her with her damn sling while I take this call."

"Yeah, do you. I got her."

"Hello."

"Hey Mignon, what's good?"

"Nothing much, who's this?"

"Richard, what, you don't have my number stored in your phone?"

"Nah, haven't had a chance for that yet. What's on your mind." Mignon asked as she turned her mouth up, due to her not really wanting to be bothered.

"Hey, Lil' Kitty just got off the phone with me talking about some guys wanted y'all up there this weekend. I told her I wanted to check with you first."

"I don't know about that, Rich. Tell you what though. I'm right in the middle of something. Can I call you back when I finish? Then I'll let you know something then."

"Cool, hit me up ASAP."

"Yeah, got to run, peace," she said as she hung up the phone. She looked over at Entyce, sitting in the passenger seat.

"So, who was that, Richard?"

"Yes girl, if you knew, why did you ask?"

"My bad chick. What's up?"

"Something about some guy calling hot ass Lil' Kitty, and saying how they want us all up there this weekend."

"So what's up, we going?"

"I really don't know right now Entyce. Something doesn't feel right. We just killed that nigga from up there, and now someone called her ass wanting us up there. I would feel better, if the team of us ladies were all together."

"I feel you on that. With Nicole in the hospital, and ole Berry in the backseat with one arm. That only leaves you and I left to protect the team."

"Yep. Hey, we'll handle that issue when we get out of the hospital. Now let's all get our composure together, so we can see our girl."

"Sounds good, let's roll." Strawberry uttered, while grimacing, trying to step out of the car.

\*\*\*

We landed in San Juan Puerto Rico, around seven that evening. After we dropped Yani back off in Miami, the flight was smooth sailing as Miguel flew the luxury jet plane back into Puerto Rico without any problems.

One we arrived in San Juan, we were greeted by a small caravan of black Range Rovers, which sped away, taking us to a very luxurious looking yacht. Then whisked away, to a small island, where Rhynyia and her family were staying.

# CHAPTER 85
## THE END!

We were then treated to a lovely array of different seafood, and fine wine, as the beautiful luxurious yacht sped across the comely looking ocean, headed to our final destination.

My brother who was living the fine life, since he had never been on a yacht or plane, couldn't resist his temptations, while eating and sucking on everything in sight, and then making sure he had a taste of everything it was to drink. I knew that our family had a lengthy history of drinking, but I only thought that it was beer, not wine. I must admit he made a believer out of me that day.

Now myself on the other hand, just sat back and tried to enjoy my short lived vacation, while chatting with Rhynyia, before reaching the island.

"So, do you always have this many bodyguards around you?" I asked her, as we both sat, sucking on Lobster Tails, drenched in butter, along with Shrimp Scampi, and giant Crab Legs.

"Not really, there more of them at the house. Let me tell you why we have so many. Since the death of my brother, my father insisted that we needed more security, to make sure we're safe at all times."

"I see. So, is that the island up ahead?" I said as I pointed up ahead at the beautiful island.

"Yes. That's exactly where we're going Michael," she said, as she put down her food, and then looked me directly in my eyes, and said. "Michael, promise me one thing while you're here?"

"What's that young lady?" I asked, as I placed my napkin back down between my legs.

"Don't, I mean no matter how tempting the offer is, no matter how much money it is, please don't get involved in my father's business."

"Rhynyia, like I told you on the phone before coming here. I promise that I won't get involved with your father. Drugs are not something that I partake into," I replied, as I kissed her on the lips, while she sat there, with what looked like a tear in her eye.

I then sat back, searching her face for answers, not knowing that it was my dear brother, who she had to worry about. Eating and drinking like his ass hadn't ate anything in two full days.

In the end, it would be Rhynyia and I, who had to pay for his deadly mistake. Little did we both know it at the time, my dear older brother Firstborn was headed straight for disaster and we never saw it coming. If only we would have had some type of warning before we allowed him to accompany us to Puerto Rico, maybe the ending to my story would have been a more colorful one. But in life, you never see the ending until it's already right smack in front of you!

# CHAPTER 86
## LOOKING FOR MIKE!

The door of the hospital room gently slid open, as Sharon's mother stood, thinking that it was one of nurses coming to check on her.

"Hello ma'am, is she awake yet?"

"She just dozed back off to sleep. Is there something I can help you with?" her mother asked, as she stood there, not realizing who it was that she was talking too.

"No, I'm sorry to interrupt you at this time."

"It's okay, can I ask who you are?"

"Yes, sorry. I'm with the police department. I was here to see if your daughter could give us any details about what happened?" the white, tall young slender officer asked, as he painted a fake smile on his face.

"Oh I see! So you all couldn't wait until my daughter recovered from her injuries? Haven't you guys done enough damage already, without coming here to do more?"

"I'm so sorry ma'am. I can come back later. I didn't mean to disturb you or your daughter."

"Yes, why don't you do that?" her mother recited, angrily.

"No problem ma'am. Have a nice day, and I hope she has a speedy recovery."

"Thank you. Now can I please have some quiet time with my daughter!" her mother recited, as she sat back down, furious that the police department had sent someone by her daughters room so soon.

The young officer had just walked back from the hospital room. With his back falling hard up against the wall in the hallway, as he whispered out loud. *'Damn, there is no way that I'm going to allow that bitch to live. Her life will be snatched away from her, just as she snatched away the life of my dear grandmother!'*

The young officer then turned to walk away. He had just got to the entrance of the emergency room door, when his shoulder lightly bumped into the arm of one of the unsuspected Murder Queens.

"Oh, excuse me officer." Mignon uttered, as her shoulder brushed up against the officer.

"No problem ma'am, I should watch where I'm walking," he said as he turned to look at the sight of the beautiful young lady.

"Damn chick, he almost tore your arm right out of the socket!" Entyce muttered.

"Yes he did. Strawberry, c'mon man, you act like you know the damn man or something."

Strawberry was still standing at the entrance of the emergency room door, looking at the back of the officer's head, when she sluggishly turned back around and said. "I don't know about you two, but ole boy, looks just like a younger version of that one officer who came by the house looking for Mike the other day."

"Whatever, girl bring your silly ass on." Entyce shouted back at her, just as her and Mignon stopped at the front desk.

"Yes, can I help you ladies?" the day time attendant asked, as she smiled up at the ladies standing in front of her.

"Yes, we're here to see a friend of ours, her name is D Nicole Jackson."

"No problem, you said her name is Nicole Jackson. Correct?"

"Yes ma' am."

"Okay, here we go. She's located in room twelve fifteen. Take the elevator right there to the twelfth floor, and her room should be three doors down on the right side." the lady replied as her face held the same smile as before.

"Thank you, ma'am," they all said in unison while walking towards the elevator.

# CHAPTER 87
## LICKING ASS!

In Jacksonville, Florida. Marquise was busy at his rib joint, putting together his plan of attack for the ladies who had took out his brother and friend. He was confused and perturbed, thinking if he should just kill everyone that was even associated with the ladies.

How would he be able to get away with mass murder and how could he get rid of all the dead bodies that would be left behind without causing some type of panic in Jacksonville. He sat in the dark of his office, contemplating, what would be the best course of action, when his office phone rang. It immediately snapped him out of his trance, as he answered. "Hello."

"Hello. Is this Marquise Williams?"

"Yes, may I ask who's speaking?" he said, as he rolled up to his desk, trying to clear his bewildered mind.

"This is Claude, with the funeral home, I was just calling to see if you wanted the deluxe package for Rasheed as well?"

"Yes, make sure all three of them have the deluxe package. Hey, I was wondering if y'all could bury my brother in something that resembled his car?"

"His car?"

"Yes, maybe a casket, with some rims on it. You know make it as if he was going out in style."

"When were you and the family planning on burying him and the others?"

"I know my family is still trying to pick a date. As far as the other families, I don't know yet."

"Okay, let me call them. In the meantime, I'll check with some people in regards to that order for your brother."

"Thanks, call me as soon as you find out." Marquise hung up, now even more angry, due to him having to have to pay for three costly funerals.

'Damn. It's going to be hell to pay. Now that I have three people to bury!' he yelled out loud .

***

Richard's eyes were rolling in the back of his head as he sat in the driver's seat of his truck. He was owing and awing, while Lil' Kitty, slow sucked his penis. "Damn girl, now I see why my cousin has your lil' ass in the group! Yo' head is fucking fye."

"Whatever Richard, I'm in the group, because I know how to get that paper. Now shut yo' bitch ass up and hurry up and nut! I ain't about to be sucking yo' fat lil' short ass dick all day."

"Shit, you don't have to. Why don't you let me hit that ass real quick."

Her lil' head popped up real quick, as she surveyed the parking lot of the projects.

"What are you looking for?" He asked, as he sat there holding his dick.

"Trying to see if your windows are dark enough, so no one can look in here and see what we're doing."

"Fuck all of that, just slide your lil short ass in the back seat real quick. I promise you, I will be done within five minutes." he said as he smiled at the lil bush she had between her legs.

"C'mon boy, and you betta be through in five minutes.

And oh, I do won't to try out yo' fye ass head." smiling from ear to ear, he kindly replied.

"Shit, that's not a problem, while I'm at it, let me show you how good I am, when it comes to licking ass!"

# CHAPTER 88
## DOWN AND DIRTY!

"Damn Richard, I never knew that you liked to lick ass, my nigga!"

"I know, I just don't go around licking every females ass. But I sure as hell am about to lick yours. Now slide them lil ass thongs off." Just as she went to slide her thongs off, Richard was down there already between her legs, naked, with his pants dangling by his ankles.

He gently put his hands underneath her soft ass and then slid her into his mouth as he pulled her legs apart, seeing his prize up ahead. He then slid his large head in between her legs. Catching her spur tongue in between his teeth, and then tenderly pulling on it, causing her to ease her head back up against the door. Making it seem as if she had just pushed a Heroin needle into her arm, with the way her head eased back up against the door of his truck.

"Damn boy, what are you doing to me? Why does it feel like you have all of your damn tongue up in my pussy." she uttered, as her eyes rolled in the back of her head.

"Because I do. Now watch this." he then slid his long ass index finger inside her tight asshole.

"Oh shit Richard, boy you are a beast!" she recited as she tightly grabbed the back of his head, and then pushed his head deep off into her sweet smelling pussy.

He then slid his finger out of her ass, replacing it with the tip of his tongue. Then, softly entering into where no other man had ever been before.

"No-no-no." she mumbled.

But it was too late. Seconds later, his entire tongue was plunged in her small rectum, with her cumming all over his forehead.

"My bad, I couldn't help it," she said, as she tried to control her pleasure.

"No problem. I'm about to suck all that shit up. Now watch this."

He went back into her asshole, while taking his two fingers, soothingly playing with her spur tongue. He then began thrusting back and forth with his tongue in her ass as if he was fucking her ass with his long ass tongue.

"Damn Richard, here it comes again."

This time he was ready. He moved his head back up towards her pussy as she released another load of her juices into his open mouth. Just as he had licked the last bit of her secretions, he slid up on top of her, slowly inserting his four inch pipe, while wiping his mouth on the sleeve of his shirt.

"Yep, there it is." he uttered, as he smiled at her.

"What is?" she asked as she looked back at him with a confused look on her face.

"That dick. Don't act like you don't feel me all up inside yo' stomach!"

"I don't. What is that your hand?" she said as she tried to look down at his dick.

Whatever Kitty, just lay back, and take all of this meat."

"Yeah, okay."

He then did the unthinkable, as he went to place his mouth on her mouth.

"Oh hell naw. Boy you done lost yo' damn mind if you think that you about to put your mouth on my mouth after you have ate out my ass!" she screamed as she pushed him off of her.

"What? It was your ass that I just ate. You act like I ate somebody else, and then tried to kiss you."

"Boy I don't know who's ass you have been eating on. So don't think that I'm about to kiss your stank mouth ass. Now, do you want to finish trying to fuck me with that short fat ass dick, or can I have some more of that fye ass head of yours?"

"Whatever man, I'm good," he said as he moved over so he could pull up his pants. Disgusted and hurt by her comments.

"Shit, I don't know why you're mad and shit. At least I got mine."

"Fuck you, Lil Kitty!" she looked back over at him, as she fixed herself back up, looking in the mirror at the same time. Then looking back over at him.

"Nah, fuck you, ass eating ass nigga!" she then slammed his door, smiling as she sashayed her lil small hips, so that he could see what he had just licked on.

# CHAPTER 89
## SKATES BOSS!

"Damn, she looks so peaceful, laying there as if she was waiting to die."

"Strawberry please. Could you have thought of something else more serene than that cold hearted shit you just let roll off of them dick sucking ass lips of yours!" Strawberry cut a mean grimacing smile back in the direction of Mignon.

Then saying. "So I said something awful. But your pretty thick booty ass, could only think of someone sucking dick right about now."

"C'mon ladies, our girl is laying there stiff, and frozen. While y'all two bitches act a fool in her room." Strawberry stood back from the bed, still eyes glued to Mignon's head.

"Your right, Entyce. We need to act our age, not our shoe size. And besides, our girl needs us more than anything right about now."

"Thats the most intelligent thing your ass had said in the last few weeks," Mignon replied as a wicked smirk ran across her face.

"Whatever Mignon." Strawberry uttered as she stood at a distance, still feeling sorry for her girl.

"So, what's those tubes and shit running out of her arms?"

"Looks like an IV. Now them other things hooked to her chest, and on her finger, I think those are all hooked, making

243

sure they keep an eye on her heart rate and respiratory system, Entyce."

"I wonder if she's even woke up since being here?"

I have no idea. Hey Strawberry, go look and see if you can find a nurse, or a doctor, so we can at least find out how she's doing."

"Gotcha boss, right away. I could move a lil faster if I had some skates on boss," she uttered, as she turned for the door, laughing to herself.

"Alright Strawberry, keep it up."

"I'm gone man," she said as she dashed out of the door.

***

We had just arrived at the magnificent lavish estate that Rhynyia and her family called home. I mean it was huge, as Firstborn and I gazed upon the large, vast mansion, that was attached to a few other small homes as well. Rhynyia gazed at the both of us as we stood there marveling at the place. She then cut a radiant smile at the both of us as she stood in front of the house, spreading open her arms and then saying.

"Michael, welcome to my families hacienda!" Both of our mouths were still open, when suddenly, her dignified looking sisters emerged from the house, smiling from ear to ear to see Rhynyia and my brother.

They were standing in the doorway, looking just as beautiful as Rhynyia. First it was her baby sister, who went by the name of Maylia. She was a gorgeous young seventeen year old female, who stood around four foot eight inches, and weighing a hundred and fifteen pounds. With long silk brown hair, and light brown pretty eyes to go along with her charming smile.

Her second sister went by the name of Countess, who was nineteen years of age, and stood five foot two, weighing a mere hundred and twenty five pounds, with jet black hair, that laid down the small of her back.

The third sister, who was the oldest of the three, was another version of Rhynyia. Her name was Natasha, and she stood five foot eight, and looked like she weighed about a hundred and thirty five pounds. She too had very long black jet hair that she wore to the side of her splendid looking face.

# CHAPTER 90
## FAVORITE POSTION!

After several delightful minutes of Firstborn and I meeting the family, we took off headed for our different rooms. Just like my mother would have suggested if I was to bring Rhynyia to her house, we had to sleep in separate rooms, due to us not being married yet. Something I fully understood.

Now my brother, on the other hand, couldn't wait until he got to his room so he could pass out. He claimed that he was still tired from the flight, but truth be told, his ass was still tipsy from the night before. As we both followed behind the butler of the house to our individual rooms, he looked over at me and whispered.

"Hey Baby Boy, please never let me get as drunk as I did last night!"

"One should always be alert to how much alcohol one consumes," I replied, as I walked into the large room for me to sleep in.

He quickly threw up his middle finger, and shouted. "What the fuck ever!" as he stumbled head first into his room.

As I placed my bags down on the extra-large king sized bed, I threw myself along it and looked up into the ceiling before thinking to myself.

'A nigga can really get used to this type of shit!'

I was still at awe, at all the power and mystique that her family had, and to think, I was half way into the Santiago family. All I had to do now, was to just marry the most gorgeous girl in the world. Rhynyia Marisa Santiago and I would be set for life.

I just didn't know that my adversary was in the room across the hall from me, sleeping off his drunken binge. My dear old brother was about to be the first person in my life that would try to bring me down. And to think, I had no earthly idea of his diabolical plan.

I fell asleep around ten thirty and didn't wake up until around two in the morning, when Rhynyia decided to crawl in the bed with me. I densely rolled over to caress her soft tender body, as I softly whispered into her ear. "Now what if your father catches you here sleeping next to me?" she turned her head slightly and uttered.

"Michael, has anyone ever told your ass that you worry too much about nothing. I'm already pregnant and besides that, I have this big ass ring on my finger to prove to the world that I'm already yours. Plus, my father is not even here, big head."

"Okay, just don't get me killed while I'm down here in Puerto Rico. No one would ever know what ever happened to me but my immediate family.

"Shut up boy, and make sweet passionate love to me," she said as I proceeded to take out my already erect penis, and gently insert it into her from the back. Her favorite position.

***

Daytona Beach, Florida. The girls had just arrived back where it all started. Mignon turned the car off, then looking over to Entyce.

"So, ole girl is working right?"

"Yes Mignon. I told you before we left the hospital that she was. The bitch doesn't get off until eleven."

"Cool, well let's give it a minute or two, and then we'll go inside." Mignon uttered, as she surveyed the parking lot.

# CHAPTER 91
## AS WE SPEAK!

The parking lot seemed half empty as the women sat patiently waiting for the right time to embark on the building. Entyce sat calmly in the passenger seat while chewing on a piece of gum. Mignon cooly stared out of the dark tinted windows, making sure they went unnoticed.

Then without any hint or notice, Strawberry blurted from the back seat. "I hope y'all realize, that this bitch probably has twenty four hour security wrapped around her ass, since she is the only witness who knows what the hell we look like."

Entyce dimly turned her head in the direction of Mignon and said. "You know, she does have a valid point there."

"Yeah, yeah, yeah. That's what I've been thinking too. But by the time we get ready to make our move on her ass, the coast might be clear of any police protection."

"Let's hope so. Cause if not, some lucky son of a bitch, is going to be hundred thousand dollars richer, with the capture of us. Did it say dead or alive, Mignon?" Mignon hastily turned to the back seat and growled. "Does is it really matter. I ain't planning on letting no one catch my ass. Now as far as you are concerned, that's on you!"

"Hey-hey, y'all two calm down for a minute. There's ole girl right there, taking out the trash. And look, the door of the place is still open. This is our best chance right now! Let's go!"

Mignon placed her arm in front of Entyce as she mumbled. "Hold up, it looks like somebody is holding the door for her."

"Who do you think it is?"

"Hell, how am I supposed to fucking know? I don't work here. I guess it's another employee."

"Yeah, whoever it is, we need to break right now." Entyce barked as she pulled down her black mask.

"Okay, it's now or never, let's go." the three ladies quietly emerged from the car, and swiftly ran towards the open back door with their guns swinging from their arms.

Just as they got to the rear of the restaurant, Mignon held up her four nickel and barked. "Take one move and it's the last move you will ever take!" the young lady was frightened half to death, as she dropped what was in her hand and imprudently replied.

"No-no, please don't shoot me!"

"Shhhh, we ain't gonna shoot you. All we want is to walk back up in here with you nice and slow. We don't even want to rob the place. Just do as I say, and everything will be alright. Do you understand?" the frightened lady's mouth frantically began to quiver as she looked at the other two masked females and uttered.

"Yes, I hear you. Please don't hurt me. I have three young kids at home!"

"Cool. So, if you want to ever see them again, you'll do as we ask you to. Now, how many customers are still inside eating?"

"Like around ten, or maybe twelve. I really don't know."

"Okay, we already have a problem. Make up your damn mind, is it ten or twelve?" Entyce barked as she placed her Glock up under the ladies small chin.

"Oh shit! I think it's twelve."

"Good, now let me tell you what we want. Walk us nice and slow inside to the manager's office. Can you do that without startling and alerting them to us?"

"Yes, I believe so."

"Well let me tell you what's going to happen if you don't. Remember what happened to that guy last weekend?"

"Yeeeees. Yes, the guy that was shot by the four women."

"Yes. Well three of them four bad ass women are back, and you don't want a repeat show of what took place last time, do you?"

"No not at all."

"Fine. Good girl. Now get us to that office so we can watch the tape. The one lone witness has to be somewhere on the tape. She saw the culprits of that incident on that day."

"You talking about Marcy Grayson. She's the one who claims that she saw your faces."

"What?" Mignon asked, as the other two Murder Queens looked on in suspense.

"The witness. Her name is Marcy Grayson."

"How do you know that?"

"Because she's the wife of the manager!"

"What?"

"Yes, and she's inside his office with him as we speak."

# CHAPTER 92
## HOT ASS!

Mignon, nor the rest of her crew, could believe their ears, as they watched the words slowly roll off of her lips.

"So, let us get this straight. The person who saw us is the wife of the manager of this nice establishment here?" Mignon asked, as she held her victim at bay.

"Yes. She's inside right now. Along with three undercover cops, who are supposed to be protecting her," their victim said as she stood there, still terrified half to death.

"Damn, now there lies the problem. There's no way we can get to her if she's protected by three undercover cops." Entyce uttered, as she placed her head down.

"Not to mention, if I don't get back inside, someone is going to come out here looking for me."

"She's right, Mignon. What in the hell are we going to do now?" Strawberry asked as she peered around the door, wildly searching for anyone trying to be nosey.

"Hold on, let me quarterback this thing for a minute. We got this." Mignon muttered as she began rattling her brain for different scenarios.

"Please, just let me get back inside. I'll keep everyone distracted while you all come up with a plan."

"No need for that sister. Your white Lilly ass is going to get us inside the manager's office without anyone knowing a thing. If not, my girl here with the itchy finger is going to go to your home and take care of your kids for you! Do you understand?" Mignon barked, as the frightened young lady gladly agreed on what was said.

"Yes, I'll do whatever it is you need me to do, just don't hurt me or my kids."

"Fine, let's move. " Mignon ordered as she then looked over at Entyce and Strawberry. "Okay, listen ladies, the only way we're getting in here unnoticed is by us taking off these fucking masks."

"But our identity will be seen." Strawberry griped, with a quizzical look on her face.

"Not if we all walk in at different times with our faces hidden from view. Watch closely and follow my lead. Now let's move young lady," Mignon said as her and the victim slowly entered through the back door, desperately trying to go unnoticed, to the other employees or the three unsuspected cops. Who by the way things looked, seemed to be to occupied by what was flashing on the television screen.

\*\*\*

Meanwhile, Lil' Kitty had grown impatient with finding out if they were all going to Jacksonville for the weekend. So she called Richard back, as she paced her bedroom, still feeling the after effects of the Kush weed that she had been smoking on all day.

His phone rung one time, as he dully rolled over and answered it on the very first ring.

"Yeah Lil' Kitty, what is it now?"

She smiled out loud as she came back over the phone with. "What, I know you ain't still mad at me, about earlier?"

"Whatever, I like the way you tried to play me today after I ate your pussy and licked your ass!" he angrily said, as he laid there in bed, still irritated with her for not letting him bust his nut, or kiss her in the mouth.

"C'mon Richard, stop it. Who in their right mind, let's a nigga kiss them in the mouth, after they have licked that person's crack in their ass. Now be serious. At least I didn't say that I didn't like the way you ate my ass and licked this pussy!" she stated, as a smile spread across the face of the booty eating bandit.

'Whatever, my baby mamma never complained, when I ate her ass, and then kissed her." he uttered, as Lil' Kitty took the phone from her mouth and whispered to herself. *'Uggh, that's why Do-Dirty's mouth, always smelt like hot ass!*

# CHAPTER 93

## IN THE FIRST PLACE!

Lil Kitty was still stewing about the thought of even letting his mouth get close to hers, when she came back over the phone with. "Okay, enough of the booty eating shit, are we going to Jacksonville this weekend, or what?"

"Mignon never called me back," Richard said, as he raised up in bed.

"So why didn't you call her back? I really need to know what's up."

"I'll find out first thing in the morning. Once I find out, you'll be the first female I call."

"You betta call me too, Richard. I have to call my boo back to let him know we're coming."

"Everybody is your boo."

"Bye Richard.

*Click*." the phone hung up, just as Richard, uttered. "Bitch."

\*\*\*

The door of the manager's office opened up hazily, as the young employee emerged from around the door. "Excuse me Brad, but there's someone here who needs to speak with you," she said as she stepped in the door way of the small office.

Brad looked up jolted as he said. "Jody, you see that I'm doing the count of the money drawers. What could be that important that you have to interrupt me right now?"

"This is, muthafucker. Close your mouth, and shut the fuck up!" Mignon yelped as she came through the open door, weapon in hand, pointed directly in his face.

"Oh shit, what in the name of God." Brad yelled as he fumbled around his desk. "You know what it is, don't make a move, or the fat bitch that can't keep her mouth quiet gets two bullets right in the front of her fucking head!" Mignon recited, as Brad looked over at his scared shitless wife.

"Honey don't move, everything will be okay. Just do as they say. Now all of the money is right here, so you don't have to hurt us."

"Man this is ain't about no damn money. It's about what your wife said to the damn cops!" Entyce voiced as she slid through the door with her gun in hand.

"Alright, now that the both of you know why we're here, this is how this is going to go down. My girl Berry is outside on the door, so don't think that your about to do something crazy. All we need is for your wife here to keep her damn mouth closed. No one will get hurt, and you will never see our faces again. Do you understand?" Mignon barked as she kept an eye on the video cameras located inside the office.

"Yes. This isn't a robbery?" he said as he sat there motionless.

"No my good man. Your wife knows exactly what this is all about. She is the only witness to what took place last week. It seems as though she went to the police and gave them a description of what the culprits looked like. What we need now is for her to keep her mouth closed. Or we will close it for her and you."

"But what about the cops? I told them everything. Now there monitoring our home and keeping us protected at all times."

"By the way it looks right now, they have slipped up.

You're here with me and my partner right now." Mignon said as Entyce, chimed in with.

"Not to mention with a fully loaded Glock pointed at your head. So the way we see it is someone is not doing their fucking job."

"She does have a point there Brad. By the way, where are those hot ass cheese biscuits?"

Mignon quickly snapped her head around, when she heard the voice of Strawberry and said. "Serious, you left the door for some damn biscuits?"

"Damn skippy, I got to have them. Shit, that's one of the reasons I wanted to come down here in the first place."

# CHAPTER 94
## PECAN TAN!

A few hours later, Rhynyia and I were headed down stairs to join the family for breakfast. Her lovely step mother was the first one to greet us, as she sat there with a bright smile over her radiant face and said. "Hola, Senor, how did you sleep last night?" I looked over at Rhynyia and then back at her step mother, and replied.

"Ola Senorita, I slept like a grown baby." smiling, as I pulled Rhynyia's chair from under the table and whispered into her ear, as she sat down on her goldmine. "Hey, do you think she knows that you slept with me last night?" she waited until I sat down, and then turned to say. "Hell if I know. And what difference does it make? Like I told you last night. I'm grown."

Her step mother stood five foot four and weighed a hundred and forty five pounds, with long curly jet black hair.

Her face held a very stern look with a very charming smile to go right along with all of her beautiful characteristics, that made her the perfect woman for the job of being married to Pierre Santiago.

She made me and my brother feel like family by the way she spoke to us. For the very first time, Firstborn actually acted like he was a gentleman, with the proper way he carried himself around her family. For a minute there, he made me proud those first few days that we were on the island. It wouldn't be until later when he changed from the nice mild mannered guy, into a self-made drug kingpin overnight, that ruled his employees and business partners like he was on top of the world.

After we all devoured the wonderful breakfast that their servants had prepared for the family, Rhynyia took my brother and I throughout the city revealing to us the different parts of her very chaotic world. The atmosphere was totally different than back in Orlando. The people in her community treated her with the utmost respect and dignity.

When the locals got close enough to her, they would always adhere to her presence. Honestly, being with her had me feeling some type of way. I guess it was due to all her fortune and fame.

My brother on the other hand kept saying to me.

"Man, I want me one too, just like her."

"Well I guess you need to go try to find you one. Because this one is all mine." I sputtered as we journeyed from store to store, looking for me and him something to wear to the funeral.

While walking hand and hand with her, I grew the stares from some of the local island men, who I guess couldn't figure out why Rhynyia had choose me over them. Funny thing about that situation, was that the local women would beg to differ, as they couldn't keep from blushing at me every time my eyes crossed theirs. I guess it was due to my five foot ten stature and the way I carried the hundred and ninety five pounds of weight. Not to mention with the way the sun, shined off of my pecan tan.

I was still throwing my signature smiles back at the women, when I happened to look down at my brothers toes, protruding out of his sandals.

"Yo' Firstborn, the next time that your country ass decides to put on a pair of sandals, please make sure that you wear some socks on them jacked up ass toes of yours!"

"Whatever, real men don't go to the nail salon and have their feet done. Pretty muthafucka!" he replied as he pulled down his Versace shades, staring me directly back in my face.

While walking down the store front plaza, he must have caught a glimpse of how he looked, when he saw his reflection in the mirrors. He quickly turned to me and shouted. "Damn Mike, who is that fine ass brother walking next to you?"

"Man you tripping off how you look today, when I look like this every day."

Rhynyia then turned to me and recited. "Yeah, I guess that's why you have a problem with keeping your dick in your pants, huh?"

We all kept quiet as she stared at me, waiting for me to answer her question.

# CHAPTER 95
## UNCLE FELIX!

My brother and I kept quiet as Rhynyia stood there staring at me, waiting for me to answer her question. After a few seconds of me standing there with my head down, as if I was a child being scolded, she blurted out. "Have you two figured out what type of suits it is that you won't to wear to my brother's funeral?"

My brother then turned to me, nudging me as he uttered. "Damn nigga, say something, it's your chick."

"Not really, can we stop at a few more stores please?"

"I guess, but first. The baby and I are hungry. Let's get something to eat before we continue shopping." she voiced, as she turned, slightly walking in front of us.

"I guess you heard that!"

"Shut up, bro. I guess that I'm not as lucky as you are when it comes to the women that you have kids by." I recited as I turned trying to keep up with Rhynyia and the guards that trailed her.

"And what is that supposed to mean lil brother?"

"In other words, your baby mamma's don't care what you do, just as long as you send them some money every now and then."

"Yep, and that's exactly how I like it."

"Good luck with them when it's time for the family reunion," I replied just as Rhynyia turned around to us and said. "Right here guys, this is my favorite place to eat at whenever I'm home."

We then walked inside the nice elegant, small eatery, as everyone turned to see that it was Rhynyia walking through the door.

We took a table by the window as her bodyguards took a table right across from us. Before we even sat down, my nose caught the nice smelling aroma of all the different foods that they were in the back cooking. That's when I leaned over, rubbing her thigh and softly asked. "So what type. of food do they serve here?"

"It's various cultures of food they have to offer here. You have your Caribbean food, and your Hispanic food as well as a bit of American food to boost. This Cafe is the oldest of its kind here on the island. My Uncle Felix owns the place."

"Oh really. I must admit that the place is nicely decorated. I can see myself owning something just like this one day," I replied, while having a broad smile across my face.

"Yeah, I bet you could." she voiced as she put her head into her menu.

Just as she had mumbled those words, this somewhat tall slender Puerto Rican gentleman with a full beard, trimmed up neatly on his face, began walking towards our table. He had to be at least six foot two and weighed around two hundred pounds exactly. His hair was nicely cut as it sat admirably on top of his head. By the way his knitted silk shirt clung to his chest, I could tell that the brother worked out.

*Damn, could this be a hit right here in front of all these people?* I said to myself, as the four guards that were with us stood straight up as if the man was royalty. They didn't even flinch, as the young man stood over our table, hovering us. At first I thought that he was there to take our order, or maybe take Rhynyia out without her even knowing what was going on, since he came up from the rear of her.

Me being on high alert, alerted my brother, who was busy trying to read the menu.

"Hey man, looks like we have company!" his head smoothly snapped up, but it was too late, as the man leaned over and uttered.

"Excuse me. May I take your order, Princess?" Rhynyia instantaneously turned her head as she heard the familiar voice. She tried to scream as her hands cupped her mouth, then yelling out loud. "Well hello, Uncle Felix!"

## DEADLY ADVERSARY!

A few hours earlier, back inside Sharon's room, she had woken up two hours after her mother had left the hospital. Her mind was going back and forth, between her kidnappers and the young lady's face she had seen while laying her head in her lap, after being rescued.

So many thoughts were traveling through her confused brain, when her dinner tray arrived. The evening nurse gently walked into her room, holding a tray of food, while gleaming with a radiant smile on her face.

"Good evening ma'am, I hope you're hungry?"

"Somewhat. I guess I should eat something, so I can build my strength back up," Sharon said as she pushed herself up. Then pressing the button on the cord, allowing the bed to raise up so that she could eat.

"Yes, that you do have to do. I hope you enjoy your dinner. Don't hesitate to call me if you need anything else."

"Yes ma'am, thank you," she said as she took the top off of the tray of food.

As soon as she had lifted the top, she shouted out. "What the hell? Why does everyone think that I like eating asparagus?"

The door of her room slung back open, with the nurse frantically asking her. "Is there something wrong ma'am?"

Sharon's head snapped up as she replied, "No, everything is fine. It's just that I don't like asparagus. Is their another vegetable I can have besides this one?"

"Yes ma'am, what would you like?" the young nurse asked as she walked back towards her bed, still holding onto that radiant smile.

"Yes. Do they have some corn, or maybe corn on the cob?"

"Yes, they do. I will be right back with some corn. Now let me get this out of your way."

"Thank you."

"Don't mention it, ma'am. That's what I'm here for; to make sure that everything is okay," the young nurse recited as she went for the door.

Sharon then took a small bite out of the roasted chicken as she turned the volume up on her television. She had just begun enjoying her meal when she heard the news reporter talking about her ordeal.

"Yeah, I hope them bastards all died!" she uttered as she took a sip of her tea.

It wasn't until she heard the reporter say that two of the five officers were still alive, and at the same hospital she was at. Her fork fell hard to her tray, clanking as she laid back, saying to herself, "No the hell they ain't here! Well I hope their ass is ready for some muthafucking payback, because bitch it's on!"

As soon as she said that, the door of her room slid open. "Did you say something, ma'am?"

"No, not at all. Is this the corn?"

"Yes, ma'am."

"Thank you."

"No problem. Here you are." The young lady then handed the saucer full of corn to her, and turned for the door. "Oh, by the way, ma'am. My shift is over, but your nighttime nurse will be around to check on you later tonight."

"Thank you. Have a nice night," Sharon said as the young lady disappeared out of the room, leaving Sharon to thinking of how she would finally dispose of her deadly adversary.

# CHAPTER 96
## LET ME HELP YOU!

Her nighttime nurse had just given her the final dose of her evening medication. Sharon pretended to have taken them as she watched the nurse leave the room. She leaped out of bed, placing her head close to the door, making sure her nurse was far away as she slid out of the room.

She then briskly walked down the hallway, searching for the nurses' closet. Once inside, she speedily snatched off her gown, trading it for a tight-fitting nurse's uniform. Once she made sure it was a nice fit, she stepped out in search of the lone room that held the man responsible for her and her daughter's kidnapping. She cool and ubiquitously walked to the unoccupied nurses' station and retrieved the information needed and then proceeded to Lieutenant Richards' room with one thing on her mind. Revenge.

She walked right past the nighttime security guards into his room as the unsuspected victim shyly rolled over to get a good glimpse of the nurse that was on duty for the night due to him always feeling her up, trying to get his rocks off. But tonight, he would get more than just a feel of some female's nice ass legs. For tonight he would get his ultimate death wish while she would get her revenge by taking his life.

As the beautiful red female got closer to his bed, Lieutenant Richards stuck his hand out as usual, desperately trying to reach for the nurse's leg that seemed to be a shade bit darker this evening.

When she saw his partially badly burned face underneath his bed sheets, she quickly grabbed him by his left arm, and looked him directly in his cold, dark blue eyes. "Remember me, bitch?"

He then looked up into her menacing big brown eyes as she ground her teeth with hatred in her heart towards the man.

"You stank ass, asparagus-eating muthafucka. You're going to die for real tonight."

Seeing who it was, he wildly began trying to keep the young lady from taking him out, as he recklessly fought with her, fearing for his dear life.

Sharon hadn't anticipated the struggle that ensued as she daringly tried to subdue the heavy-handed man. Two minutes had elapsed as she tried to inject the deadly poison she had into his IV.

Just as she seen that it was now do or die, the damn door to his room slid open. *Oh shit, the security guard is about to come in*, she thought as she began to panic.

Fearing that she was about to be caught trying to kill an officer of the law, she mumbled to herself there was no way in hell she was going to spend the rest of her life behind bars for such a hideous crime. So she quickly put the syringe back in her pocket and tried to make it seem as though she was working.

As she hastily turned to look at who was coming through the door, she was shocked to witness his nighttime nurse, walking towards his bed with her back turned. Thinking quick on her feet, she tried to walk past the real nurse, and would have gotten away until the unthinkable happened. The poisoned filled syringe fell out of her pocket and rolled right onto the oncoming nurse's foot.

Sharon froze right dab smack in her tracks; the syringe would have never fallen out of her pocket if her nervous hand hadn't been fumbling around in the tight fitted outfit. Carelessly tremblingly, she bent down to retrieve the syringe as it rolled directly in front of the nurse who was standing over her head.

The nurse saw the syringe and bent over herself, saying, "Here, let me help you with that."

# CHAPTER 97
## NICE ASSET!

Sharon noticed something very unusual for a nurse. She was wearing red bottom heels. Something that a nurse wouldn't be wearing due to the long and strenuous hours she would be required to work.

Without thinking twice, she quickly scooped the syringe off the floor before the nurse could see it. "Why thank you, but no thanks. I got it. I seem to be so clumsy at times," Sharon said to the nurse as she wittily stood up, saying to herself, *Damn, I'm gonna have to kill this nosey ass bitch, right along with his nasty, dirty skin smelling ass!*

Just as Sharon was face to face with the nurse, she was shocked to see who the other nurse was. The nurse was just as shocked as Sharon was when she shouted out. "Sharon, what in the hell are you doing here, chick?"

"Whatever, chick. I should be asking you the same damn thing," Sharon asked as they looked at one another with the intentions of killing Lieutenant Richards in their deadly eyes.

While they were asking one another why the other was there, Lieutenant Richards was laying there with his cold blue eyes as big as fuck, wondering where in the hell the guards were who were supposed to be guarding his room. Before he could even muster up enough strength to call for the guard, both women thought quick on their feet as they took the pillow from under his head and then placed it over his badly burned face.

As the two very determined, angry black women applied great force and pressure to the pillow, it was Nicole who whispered softly in his ear, "Death is calling for yo' stank white ass."

The cold blue eyes of the hairy armed gentleman fell to his side for the very last time.

With sweat covered over the gorgeous face of Sharon, she looked up at Nicole and said, "I can't believe that you had the same thing in mind as I did."

"Nah, I can't believe that you had it in you, girl!" Nicole voiced as she wiped the sweat from her lil' button nose and then revealing a wicked, evil grin.

"Hell, if yo' ass would have been where I have been for the last few days, your mind would've caused you to do whatever it was to be free, too."

They then walked out of the room, making the crime scene look as though the man in the bed was fast asleep. They walked past the guards who were too busy checking out their bodies to even realize that the man residing in room 1242 had expired. Once back at her room, Nicole took a good look at Sharon and thought, *This bitch could have been a good fit for the Murder Queens!*

Sharon saw the way Nicole was staring at her and quickly asked, "Why are you looking at me like that?"

"Like what, chick?" Nicole asked as she smiled back at Sharon.

"Like the way you're looking. Like you have something else up your sleeve."

"Sharon, please. It's nothing chick. By the way, when are you checking out?"

"Sometime tomorrow. Hey, do me a favor. Don't let anyone know what took place here tonight."

"Hey, your secret is my secret. And besides, I owed you one. Now, sleep tight, chick," Nicole sputtered, with a smile.

"For what?"

"For all the times that you were at the house and I never said hello."

"Girl, don't mention it. Thanks for being there for me."

"Not a problem. Once I seen what you had went through on the news, I felt like I owed it to you."

"That's my girl," Sharon replied.

"Whatever. Take care."

"Will do. Now, when do you leave, chick?"

"I think tomorrow. I'm not sure."

"Okay. Talk at cha later, sis," Sharon replied as she walked away smiling to herself. She mumbled under her breath, "You know, Nicole could've been a nice asset to the Murder Queens."

## TO BE CONTINUED

## Lock Down Publications and Ca$h Presents
## Assisted Publishing Packages

| BASIC PACKAGE | UPGRADED PACKAGE |
|---|---|
| $499 | $800 |
| Editing | Typing |
| Cover Design | Editing |
| Formatting | Cover Design |
| | Formatting |
| **ADVANCE PACKAGE** | **LDP SUPREME PACKAGE** |
| $1,200 | $1,500 |
| Typing | Typing |
| Editing | Editing |
| Cover Design | Cover Design |
| Formatting | Formatting |
| Copyright registration | Copyright registration |
| Proofreading | Proofreading |
| Upload book to Amazon | Set up Amazon account |
| | Upload book to Amazon |
| | Advertise on LDP, Amazon and Facebook Page |

***Other services available upon request.
Additional charges may apply

**Lock Down Publications**
P.O. Box 944
Stockbridge, GA 30281-9998
Phone: 470 303-9761

# Submission Guideline

Submit the first three chapters of your completed manuscript to ldpsubmissions@gmail.com. In the subject line add **Your Book's Title**. The manuscript must be in a Word Doc file and sent as an attachment. Document should be in Times New Roman, double spaced, and in size 12 font. Also, provide your synopsis and full contact information. If sending multiple submissions, they must each be in a separate email.

Have a story but no way to send it electronically? You can still submit to LDP/Ca$h Presents. Send in the first three chapters, written or typed, of your completed manuscript to:

**LDP: Submissions Dept**
P.O. Box 944
Stockbridge, GA 30281-9998

*DO NOT send original manuscript. Must be a duplicate.* Provide your synopsis and a cover letter containing your full contact information.

Thanks for considering LDP and Ca$h Presents.

# NEW RELEASES

BLOODLINE OF A SAVAGE **BY PRINCE A. TAUHID**

THE MURDER QUEENS 4 **BY MICHAEL GALLON**

THE BUTTERFLY MAFIA **BY FUMIYA PAYNE**

KING KILLA 2 **BY VINCENT "VITTO" HOLLOWAY**

BABY, I'M WINTERTIME COLD 3 **BY MEESHA**

THESE VICIOUS STREETS **BY PRINCE A. TAUHID**

TIL DEATH 2 **BY ARYANNA**

CITY OF SMOKE 2 **BY MOLOTTI**

STEPPERS **BY KING RIO**

THE LANE **BY KEN-KEN SPENCE**

MONEY GAME 2 **BY SMOOVE DOLLA**

THE BLACK DIAMOND CARTEL **BY SAYNOMORE**

CRIME BOSS 2 **BY PLAYA RAY**

THUG OF SPADES **BY COREY ROBINSON**

LOVE IN THE TRENCHES 2 **BY COREY ROBINSON**

TIL DEATH 3 **BY ARYANNA**

THE BIRTH OF A GANGSTER 4 **BY DELMONT PLAYER**

PRODUCT OF THE STREETS **BY DEMOND "MONEY" ANDERSON**

# Coming Soon from Lock Down Publications/Ca$h Presents

BLOOD OF A BOSS VI
SHADOWS OF THE GAME II
TRAP BASTARD II
By **Askari**

LOYAL TO THE GAME IV
By **T.J. & Jelissa**

TRUE SAVAGE VIII
MIDNIGHT CARTEL IV
DOPE BOY MAGIC IV
CITY OF KINGZ III
NIGHTMARE ON SILENT AVE II
THE PLUG OF LIL MEXICO II
CLASSIC CITY II
By **Chris Green**

BLAST FOR ME III
A SAVAGE DOPEBOY III
CUTTHROAT MAFIA III
DUFFLE BAG CARTEL VII
HEARTLESS GOON VI
By **Ghost**

A HUSTLER'S DECEIT III
KILL ZONE II
BAE BELONGS TO ME III
TIL DEATH II
By **Aryanna**

KING OF THE TRAP III
By **T.J. Edwards**

GORILLAZ IN THE BAY V
3X KRAZY III
STRAIGHT BEAST MODE III
By **De'Kari**

KINGPIN KILLAZ IV
STREET KINGS III
PAID IN BLOOD III
CARTEL KILLAZ IV
DOPE GODS III
By **Hood Rich**

SINS OF A HUSTLA II
By **ASAD**

YAYO V
BRED IN THE GAME 2
By **S. Allen**

THE STREETS WILL TALK II
By **Yolanda Moore**

SON OF A DOPE FIEND III
HEAVEN GOT A GHETTO III
SKI MASK MONEY III
By **Renta**

LOYALTY AIN'T PROMISED III
By **Keith Williams**

I'M NOTHING WITHOUT HIS LOVE II
SINS OF A THUG II
TO THE THUG I LOVED BEFORE II
IN A HUSTLER I TRUST II
By **Monet Dragun**

QUIET MONEY IV
EXTENDED CLIP III
THUG LIFE IV
By **Trai'Quan**

THE STREETS MADE ME IV
By **Larry D. Wright**

IF YOU CROSS ME ONCE III
ANGEL V
By **Anthony Fields**

THE STREETS WILL NEVER CLOSE IV
By **K'ajji**

HARD AND RUTHLESS III
KILLA KOUNTY IV
By **Khufu**

MONEY GAME III
By **Smoove Dolla**

MURDA WAS THE CASE III
**Elijah R. Freeman**

AN UNFORESEEN LOVE IV
BABY, I'M WINTERTIME COLD III
By **Meesha**

QUEEN OF THE ZOO III
By **Black Migo**

CONFESSIONS OF A JACKBOY III
By **Nicholas Lock**

JACK BOYS VS DOPE BOYS IV
A GANGSTA'S QUR'AN V
COKE GIRLZ II
COKE BOYS II
LIFE OF A SAVAGE V
CHI'RAQ GANGSTAS V
SOSA GANG III
BRONX SAVAGES II
BODYMORE KINGPINS II
By **Romell Tukes**

KING KILLA II
By **Vincent "Vitto" Holloway**

BETRAYAL OF A THUG III
By **Fre$h**

THE MURDER QUEENS III
By **Michael Gallon**

THE BIRTH OF A GANGSTER III
By **Delmont Player**

TREAL LOVE II
By **Le'Monica Jackson**

FOR THE LOVE OF BLOOD III
By **Jamel Mitchell**

RAN OFF ON DA PLUG II
By **Paper Boi Rari**

HOOD CONSIGLIERE III
By **Keese**

PRETTY GIRLS DO NASTY THINGS II
By **Nicole Goosby**

PROTÉGÉ OF A LEGEND III
LOVE IN THE TRENCHES II
By **Corey Robinson**

IT'S JUST ME AND YOU II
By **Ah'Million**

FOREVER GANGSTA III
By **Adrian Dulan**

GORILLAZ IN THE TRENCHES II
By **SayNoMore**

THE COCAINE PRINCESS VIII
By **King Rio**

CRIME BOSS II
By **Playa Ray**

LOYALTY IS EVERYTHING III
By **Molotti**

HERE TODAY GONE TOMORROW II
By **Fly Rock**

REAL G'S MOVE IN SILENCE II
By **Von Diesel**

GRIMEY WAYS IV
By **Ray Vinci**

# Available Now

RESTRAINING ORDER I & II
By **CA$H & Coffee**

LOVE KNOWS NO BOUNDARIES I II & III
By **Coffee**

RAISED AS A GOON I, II, III & IV
BRED BY THE SLUMS I, II, III
BLAST FOR ME I & II
ROTTEN TO THE CORE I II III
A BRONX TALE I, II, III
DUFFLE BAG CARTEL I II III IV V VI
HEARTLESS GOON I II III IV V
A SAVAGE DOPEBOY I II
DRUG LORDS I II III
CUTTHROAT MAFIA I II
KING OF THE TRENCHES
By **Ghost**

LAY IT DOWN I & II
LAST OF A DYING BREED I II
BLOOD STAINS OF A SHOTTA I & II III
By **Jamaica**

LOYAL TO THE GAME I II III
LIFE OF SIN I, II III
By **TJ & Jelissa**

IF LOVING HIM IS WRONG…I & II
LOVE ME EVEN WHEN IT HURTS I II III
By **Jelissa**

BLOODY COMMAS I & II
SKI MASK CARTEL I, II & III
KING OF NEW YORK I II, III IV V
RISE TO POWER I II III
COKE KINGS I II III IV V
BORN HEARTLESS I II III IV
KING OF THE TRAP I II
By **T.J. Edwards**

WHEN THE STREETS CLAP BACK I & II III
THE HEART OF A SAVAGE I II III IV
MONEY MAFIA I II
LOYAL TO THE SOIL I II III
By **Jibril Williams**

A DISTINGUISHED THUG STOLE MY HEART I II &
III
LOVE SHOULDN'T HURT I II III IV
RENEGADE BOYS I II III IV
PAID IN KARMA I II III
SAVAGE STORMS I II III
AN UNFORESEEN LOVE I II III
BABY, I'M WINTERTIME COLD I II
By **Meesha**

A GANGSTER'S CODE I &, II III
A GANGSTER'S SYN I II III
THE SAVAGE LIFE I II III
CHAINED TO THE STREETS I II III
BLOOD ON THE MONEY I II III
A GANGSTA'S PAIN I II III
By **J-Blunt**

PUSH IT TO THE LIMIT
By **Bre' Hayes**

BLOOD OF A BOSS I, II, III, IV, V
SHADOWS OF THE GAME
TRAP BASTARD
By **Askari**

THE STREETS BLEED MURDER I, II & III
THE HEART OF A GANGSTA I II& III
By **Jerry Jackson**

CUM FOR ME I II III IV V VI VII VIII
An **LDP Erotica Collaboration**

BRIDE OF A HUSTLA I II & II
THE FETTI GIRLS I, II& III
CORRUPTED BY A GANGSTA I, II III, IV
BLINDED BY HIS LOVE
THE PRICE YOU PAY FOR LOVE I, II ,III
DOPE GIRL MAGIC I II III
By **Destiny Skai**

WHEN A GOOD GIRL GOES BAD
By **Adrienne**

A GANGSTER'S REVENGE I II III & IV
THE BOSS MAN'S DAUGHTERS I II III IV V
A SAVAGE LOVE  I & II
BAE BELONGS TO ME I II
A HUSTLER'S DECEIT I, II, III
WHAT BAD BITCHES DO I, II, III
SOUL OF A MONSTER I II III
KILL ZONE
A DOPE BOY'S QUEEN I II III
TIL DEATH
By **Aryanna**

THE COST OF LOYALTY I II III
**By Kweli**

A KINGPIN'S AMBITION
A KINGPIN'S AMBITION **II**
I MURDER FOR THE DOUGH
By **Ambitious**

TRUE SAVAGE I II III IV V VI VII
DOPE BOY MAGIC I, II, III
MIDNIGHT CARTEL I II III
CITY OF KINGZ I II
NIGHTMARE ON SILENT AVE
THE PLUG OF LIL MEXICO II
CLASSIC CITY
By **Chris Green**

A DOPEBOY'S PRAYER
By **Eddie "Wolf" Lee**

THE KING CARTEL I, II & III
By **Frank Gresham**

THESE NIGGAS AIN'T LOYAL I, II & III
By **Nikki Tee**

GANGSTA SHYT I II &III
By **CATO**

THE ULTIMATE BETRAYAL
By **Phoenix**

BOSS'N UP I, II & III
By **Royal Nicole**

I LOVE YOU TO DEATH
By **Destiny J**

I RIDE FOR MY HITTA
I STILL RIDE FOR MY HITTA
By **Misty Holt**

LOVE & CHASIN' PAPER
By **Qay Crockett**

TO DIE IN VAIN
SINS OF A HUSTLA
By **ASAD**

BROOKLYN HUSTLAZ
By **Boogsy Morina**

BROOKLYN ON LOCK I & II
By **Sonovia**

GANGSTA CITY
By **Teddy Duke**

A DRUG KING AND HIS DIAMOND I & II III
A DOPEMAN'S RICHES
HER MAN, MINE'S TOO I, II
CASH MONEY HO'S
THE WIFEY I USED TO BE I II
PRETTY GIRLS DO NASTY THINGS
**By Nicole Goosby**

LIPSTICK KILLAH I, II, III
CRIME OF PASSION I II & III
FRIEND OR FOE I II III
By **Mimi**

TRAPHOUSE KING I II & III
KINGPIN KILLAZ I II III
STREET KINGS I II
PAID IN BLOOD I II
CARTEL KILLAZ I II III
DOPE GODS I II
By **Hood Rich**

STEADY MOBBN' I, II, III
THE STREETS STAINED MY SOUL I II III
By **Marcellus Allen**

WHO SHOT YA I, II, III
SON OF A DOPE FIEND I II
HEAVEN GOT A GHETTO I II
SKI MASK MONEY I II
By **Renta**

GORILLAZ IN THE BAY I II III IV
TEARS OF A GANGSTA I II
3X KRAZY I II
STRAIGHT BEAST MODE I II
By **DE'KARI**

TRIGGADALE I II III
MURDA WAS THE CASE I II
By **Elijah R. Freeman**

THE STREETS ARE CALLING
By **Duquie Wilson**

SLAUGHTER GANG I II III
RUTHLESS HEART I II III
By **Willie Slaughter**

GOD BLESS THE TRAPPERS I, II, III
THESE SCANDALOUS STREETS I, II, III
FEAR MY GANGSTA I, II, III IV, V
THESE STREETS DON'T LOVE NOBODY I, II
BURY ME A G I, II, III, IV, V
A GANGSTA'S EMPIRE I, II, III, IV
THE DOPEMAN'S BODYGAURD I II
THE REALEST KILLAZ I II III
THE LAST OF THE OGS I II III
By **Tranay Adams**

MARRIED TO A BOSS I II III
By **Destiny Skai & Chris Green**

KINGZ OF THE GAME I II III IV V VI VII
CRIME BOSS
By **Playa Ray**

FUK SHYT
By **Blakk Diamond**

DON'T F#CK WITH MY HEART I II
By **Linnea**

ADDICTED TO THE DRAMA I II III
IN THE ARM OF HIS BOSS II
By **Jamila**

YAYO I II III IV
A SHOOTER'S AMBITION I II
BRED IN THE GAME
By **S. Allen**

LOYALTY AIN'T PROMISED I II
By **Keith Williams**

TRAP GOD I II III
RICH $AVAGE I II III
MONEY IN THE GRAVE I II III
By **Martell Troublesome Bolden**

FOREVER GANGSTA I II
GLOCKS ON SATIN SHEETS I II
By **Adrian Dulan**

TOE TAGZ I II III IV
LEVELS TO THIS SHYT I II
IT'S JUST ME AND YOU
By **Ah'Million**

KINGPIN DREAMS I II III
RAN OFF ON DA PLUG
By **Paper Boi Rari**

CONFESSIONS OF A GANGSTA I II III IV
CONFESSIONS OF A JACKBOY I II
By **Nicholas Lock**

I'M NOTHING WITHOUT HIS LOVE
SINS OF A THUG
TO THE THUG I LOVED BEFORE
A GANGSTA SAVED XMAS
IN A HUSTLER I TRUST
By **Monet Dragun**

QUIET MONEY I II III
THUG LIFE I II III
EXTENDED CLIP I II
A GANGSTA'S PARADISE
By **Trai'Quan**

CAUGHT UP IN THE LIFE I II III
THE STREETS NEVER LET GO I II III
By **Robert Baptiste**

NEW TO THE GAME I II III
MONEY, MURDER & MEMORIES I II III
By **Malik D. Rice**

CREAM I II III
THE STREETS WILL TALK
By **Yolanda Moore**

LIFE OF A SAVAGE I II III IV
A GANGSTA'S QUR'AN I II III IV
MURDA SEASON I II III
GANGLAND CARTEL I II III
CHI'RAQ GANGSTAS I II III IV
KILLERS ON ELM STREET I II III
JACK BOYZ N DA BRONX I II III
A DOPEBOY'S DREAM I II III
JACK BOYS VS DOPE BOYS I II III
COKE GIRLZ
COKE BOYS
SOSA GANG I II
BRONX SAVAGES
BODYMORE KINGPINS
By **Romell Tukes**

THE STREETS MADE ME I II III
By **Larry D. Wright**

CONCRETE KILLA I II III
VICIOUS LOYALTY I II III
By **Kingpen**

THE ULTIMATE SACRIFICE I, II, III, IV, V, VI
KHADIFI
IF YOU CROSS ME ONCE I II
ANGEL I II III IV
IN THE BLINK OF AN EYE
By **Anthony Fields**

THE LIFE OF A HOOD STAR
By **Ca$h & Rashia Wilson**

THE STREETS WILL NEVER CLOSE I II III
By **K'ajji**

NIGHTMARES OF A HUSTLA I II III
By **King Dream**

HARD AND RUTHLESS I II
MOB TOWN 251
THE BILLIONAIRE BENTLEYS I II III
REAL G'S MOVE IN SILENCE
By **Von Diesel**

GHOST MOB
By **Stilloan Robinson**

MOB TIES I II III IV V VI
SOUL OF A HUSTLER, HEART OF A KILLER I II
GORILLAZ IN THE TRENCHES
By **SayNoMore**

BODYMORE MURDERLAND I II III
THE BIRTH OF A GANGSTER I II
By **Delmont Player**

FOR THE LOVE OF A BOSS
By **C. D. Blue**

KILLA KOUNTY I II III IV
**By Khufu**

MOBBED UP I II III IV
THE BRICK MAN I II III IV V
THE COCAINE PRINCESS I II III IV V VI VII
By **King Rio**

MONEY GAME I II
By **Smoove Dolla**

A GANGSTA'S KARMA I II III
By **FLAME**

KING OF THE TRENCHES I II III
By **GHOST & TRANAY ADAMS**

QUEEN OF THE ZOO I II
By **Black Migo**

GRIMEY WAYS I II III
By **Ray Vinci**

XMAS WITH AN ATL SHOOTER
By **Ca$h & Destiny Skai**

KING KILLA
By **Vincent "Vitto" Holloway**

BETRAYAL OF A THUG I II
By **Fre$h**

THE MURDER QUEENS I II
By **Michael Gallon**

TREAL LOVE
By **Le'Monica Jackson**

FOR THE LOVE OF BLOOD I II
By **Jamel Mitchell**

HOOD CONSIGLIERE I II
By **Keese**

PROTÉGÉ OF A LEGEND I II
LOVE IN THE TRENCHES
By **Corey Robinson**

BORN IN THE GRAVE I II III
By **Self Made Tay**

MOAN IN MY MOUTH
By **XTASY**

TORN BETWEEN A GANGSTER AND A
GENTLEMAN
By **J-BLUNT & Miss Kim**

LOYALTY IS EVERYTHING I II
By **Molotti**

HERE TODAY GONE TOMORROW
By **Fly Rock**

PILLOW PRINCESS
By **S. Hawkins**

THE MURDER QUEENS 5 | MICHAEL GALLON

SANCTIFIED AND HORNY
by **XTASY**

THE PLUG OF LIL MEXICO 2
by **CHRIS GREEN**

THE BLACK DIAMOND CARTEL
by **SAYNOMORE**

THE BIRTH OF A GANGSTER 3
by **DELMONT PLAYER**

# BOOKS BY LDP'S CEO, CA$H

TRUST IN NO MAN
TRUST IN NO MAN 2
TRUST IN NO MAN 3
BONDED BY BLOOD
SHORTY GOT A THUG
THUGS CRY
THUGS CRY 2
THUGS CRY 3
TRUST NO BITCH
TRUST NO BITCH 2
TRUST NO BITCH 3
TIL MY CASKET DROPS
RESTRAINING ORDER
RESTRAINING ORDER 2
IN LOVE WITH A CONVICT
LIFE OF A HOOD STAR
XMAS WITH AN ATL SHOOTER